IT ALL STARTED
WITH A BICYCLE?

Plum McCauley

PLUM MCCAULEY

Outskirts Press, Inc.
Denver, Colorado

Outskirts Press, Inc.
http://www.outskirtspress.com

ISBN: 978-1-4327-7412-7

Outskirts Press and the "OP" logo are trademarks belonging to Outskirts Press, Inc.

PRINTED IN THE UNITED STATES OF AMERICA

Acknowledgments

I would like to thank Emil R. Salvini for his permission
to quote from his own wonderful book on Cape May,
The Summer City by the Sea,
published by Wheal-Grace Corp.

To Emma

Thank you for the greatest gift of all—a love of reading.

Chapter One

Pam sprang out of bed in a sudden burst of energy the very second she was awake. Hurrying into her fluffy green slippers, she bounded out of her bedroom door as if her room were on fire.

Today she was going back to the candy store on the boardwalk to let the owner know in person that her parents had agreed to let her "stand in" for her friend that summer. It had taken all of her powers of persuasion to convince her parents that, at eleven, she was old enough for what amounted to a part-time job. But at last she'd triumphed. She was finally going to be making more money than just her puny allowance, and in addition, she'd be helping her friend Katy.

Katy played sports at school like nobody's business. And this summer she was going away to a special camp where she'd practice all day and get even better. The only problem was, the camp was far away, and every summer Katy normally helped her parents out in their candy store by standing in front of the store with a tray of fudge, handing out samples. She had been all down in the dumps about what to do, regretting having to let her parents down, almost at the verge of changing her mind about going away, when suddenly Pam came up with the solution. *She* would take Katy's place and stand in front of the store with the tray of samples if Katy's parents wouldn't mind giving *her* the allowance for doing it that they normally gave to Katy.

Both kids were jumping for joy with their solution and descended on Katy's parents like two tornados. After a lot of serious talk, Katy's parents agreed that Pam could do the work if Katy didn't mind giving up that portion of her allowance. They also wanted to be sure that Pam's parents would understand that it wasn't an official job (because, after all, Pam was only eleven) but rather a favor.

After a lot of animated discussion when she got home, during which Pam assured her parents that she'd treat working at the candy shop as seriously as if it were a real job, they finally gave their consent, and phoned Katy's parents to let them know it was all right. Now all that remained was for Pam to find out when she could start. She just couldn't wait.

She took the first flight of stairs in record time, even by her own standards, and rushed through the hallway of the second floor of the rambling Victorian house. She very nearly barreled into Mike, the teenager who worked for her parents as a housekeeper and general handyman during the summer months that their seaside bed-and-breakfast was open to vacationers.

"Whoaho, Dude! Like, you nearly made me drop this stuff!"

"Sorry, Dude, but, like, I'm in a hurry!" Pam retorted, making fun of the way Mike spoke. She swallowed the next flight of stairs in a single rush of air.

"Dude! Watch out!" Mike called after her. "One of these days you're gonna, like, miss a step or something!" Mike entered the guest room and deposited the pile of linens on the bed. "And I'll have to clean it up, probably. Yuk."

In no time, Pam was seated at the big, round, wooden table that sat in the large bay window of the kitchen, eating the hearty breakfast that her mom had prepared. The family always ate there, for the formal dining room was reserved for their paying guests in the summer, and in the winter, the kitchen was the coziest room in the house. It was huge and old-fashioned, and the table sat in a cozy niche with a nice view of the house next door.

As Pam sat there cramming eggs, sausage, and toast into her mouth as if it were her last meal on earth, she looked out the window into the next yard, and stared at the house next door absent-mindedly, like always. At this moment, if anyone had told her that she was going to become intimately involved with that house, its history, and especially its present owners, she would have laughed out loud. Right now, it was just another fixture in the familiar landscape, inseparable from the trees, the lawn, and the garden that she knew so well.

"Pam, slow down. The store's not even open yet," her mother said as she put her hand gently on Pam's arm just as it was about to shovel another load.

Pam laughed. She laughed at everything, her white teeth showing up first in a big grin, warning that peals of laughter were shortly to follow. These teeth, almost always on display because she thought so much was funny, contrasted with the even brownness of her skin, hair, and eyes. In fact, she was almost all one color— a uniform shade of caramel, light in winter, a shade darker in summer.

"And," Pam's mother added, putting her hand once more on her daughter's arm, "you have your chores to do anyway."

"I knoooow!" Pam said impatiently. "But the faster I eat, the sooner I'll get through the chores, and the sooner I'll be at the store learning about my very first job, and so on, and so on." Really. How come parents can never see the basic logic of things?

Pam's mother gave her a sidelong glance, and continued eating.

Weeding was definitely the worst of her chores, and, unfortunately, it was also the chore she did most regularly. Although her mother's garden was lovely, especially in June when everything was just starting to come to life, the work it took to keep it up was really something. But today, Pam raced through it. All she could think about was her new job, the money she'd earn, and how she'd spend it.

It would all go toward a bike. Another bike. Another brand new, beautiful bike complete with a basket--and this time, a better lock. It would also be nice if it, too, were green, but she realized that she just might not find one exactly like the one she had. In fact, Pam thought she had better try to reconcile herself to a different color, so as she weeded, she tried to focus on the entire color spectrum in the shape of bikes. But unfortunately, despite her efforts, the bike she was picturing to herself stubbornly remained a bright shade of Kelly green.

Which, of course, only brought back painful memories of the bike she had only possessed for two short weeks at the very end of last summer. She had purchased it with her allowance savings that she had earned for two years of chores around the house. And the day she and her father brought it home was the proudest day of her life. All that work had finally paid off, and she positively treasured that bike. And then, after a mere two weeks of glorious freedom biking around town, she had come out one morning to find that it was gone--stolen right out of their driveway.

Pam recalled her disbelief as she stood there looking at the side of the house at the empty space where she had propped up her bike. Frantically, she had searched all around, looking on both sides of the house, at the back, even in unlikely places like under bushes, where it couldn't possibly be. To no avail. The shock and disappointment were incredible. It took two days for her to accept that it was actually gone.

But she was not going to wait another two years for a bike, nor was she going to wait even till the end of summer. With this new boost to her earnings, she estimated that she'd have a new bike by midsummer, if all went well. And she fully intended that all would go well.

Soon the weeding was done, and Pam raced back indoors to change clothes, almost colliding with her father and the can of paint he was carrying.

"Sorry Dad," Pam threw over her shoulder halfway up the stairs.

Mr. Fischer just shook his head, and headed out the door.

Up on the boardwalk, which ran alongside the beach for over two miles, a freshly scrubbed Pam stood hesitantly outside the door of *The Chocolate Pot*, suddenly feeling nervous and a little less confident.

What if Katy's parents weren't as nice as they seemed?

She stood looking at the shop window with its colorful display of candies, and its large copper pot, inside of which fabulous fudge of all different flavors was whipped to scrumptious perfection. Just thinking about all those flavors made Pam's mouth water. She pushed hard on the door, and went in.

The thick scent of chocolate mingled with the lighter, spicier scents of all different sorts of candies. Licorice, taffies, mints, pinwheels, butter creams, sponges, bark, gummies, lollipops, malted milk balls and hard candies of all shapes and colors were arrayed in glass jars and behind cases, the whole room as colorful and cheerful as a jar of gumdrops. Pam was suddenly much more enthusiastic.

She looked around for someone to introduce herself to, and noticed that there was a short, older woman peering at her between jars of taffy. Her eyes looked hard and glassy, and the look she gave Pam was not friendly. "Well?" the old woman asked gruffly.

Pam felt nervous again, swallowed hard, and said the first thing that came to mind.

"Could I see the manager, please?"

"What manager? We don't have a manager. I'm the manager. Who do you want?"

These questions were spat out rapidly, and Pam hardly had time to digest one, before another was on its heels. Suddenly, she wondered if she was even in the right store. Confused, she just stood there stammering, throwing out half sentences, hoping that at some point her reason for being there would become clear, but at the same time, wondering if she even wanted to work there after all. This woman wasn't at all like Katy's parents, who had seemed so nice. Katy's father had even gone so far as to tell her to call him "Bob." Who was she? Katy's grandmother?

Suddenly, right in the middle of Pam's explanation, the old woman turned abruptly away, and disappeared into the back of the store. She returned in a few seconds with Katy's father. Pam felt relief at the sight of him. Things were going to be okay after all.

"Pam! Good to see you! I talked to your parents last night. Everything looks good to go." Bob spoke in a loud, welcoming tone of voice.

Pam nodded vigorously. "I know. But they said I can only work exactly the same hours that Katy worked," she nervously reminded him.

Bob laughed reassuringly. "That's right. Five nights a week, Wednesday through Sunday, between the hours of six and eight o'clock. You'll stand right outside the door, in front of the window, and you'll hold a tray of fudge. You won't have to work too hard to get people to try some, but what I'd like you to do," he added more seriously, "is to try and get people into the store.

That's why we give out the samples. To get people to come in and buy some. You'll be our advertising," he said patting her on the shoulder. "Get it?"

Pam nodded doubtfully, suddenly a little nervous at the responsibility. What if no one went in? What if a whole night went by, and not one person ventured into the store?

As if he had read her mind, Bob patted her again on the shoulder, and reassured her. "You'll be fine. Just smile. That gets 'em every time. Are you shy?"

Pam thought for a minute, then looked up with a grin. "I don't think so," she said wrinkling her nose, and shrugging her shoulders.

Bob threw his head back and laughed. "Well, I guess we'll have to wait and see." They then arranged the terms. Katy's allowance was five dollars an hour for two hours every night she worked. That came to a whopping fifty dollars a week! Pam's eyes bulged at the thought. She'd have that bike in no time!

She could hardly wait until Bob had finished, and after he shook hands with her, Pam bounded away, forgetting all about the mean old grouch behind the counter. All she could think about was her new bike, and how wonderful it would be riding around town this summer after all. With a bike she'd be able to explore all of her favorite haunts that took way too long to walk to, like the lighthouse, and the nature trail, and the lake at Cape May Point, the southernmost tip of New Jersey. She was so excited, she couldn't stop herself from simply running down the boardwalk toward home, as fast as her legs could carry her.

Pam burst into the yard just as her father was putting the finishing touches on the sign posted on their front lawn.

"Dad! Guess what? Guess what?" She excitedly relayed the details of her extraordinary salary.

Mr. Fischer chuckled to himself as he continued painting. "Well, that's great. Just make sure you still get everything done around here, right?"

But Pam was already off, in search of her mother.

Mr. Fischer turned back to the sign. On a white background, with pink and yellow roses decorating the border, swirly black letters spelled out

The Sea Rose Inn

Except that now, one of the letters that Mr. Fischer had been touching up looked a little bit too swirly. He sighed, shook his head, and dipped his brush into the can of paint.

Chapter Two

Pam entered her bedroom out of breath from her flight home. The room was flooded with light. The sun was streaming through the front dormer windows, reminding her that it was still mid-morning. It may have been early, but what a wonderful day so far! Pam walked aimlessly around her room, picking things up and putting them down without even really seeing them. She was full of a joyous sense of contentment. Everything seemed to be going her way!

Her bedroom was the very picture of an old-fashioned girl's bedroom. When her parents had purchased the run-down Victorian house, and then restored and decorated it, they certainly hadn't neglected Pam's room. It was wallpapered with enormous pink and red cottage roses, flowers which put those skimpy ones trying to grow in their front yard to shame. The bed, the armoire, the child's desk and bookcases, and the small rocking chair were all gleaming mahogany—the result of her father's considerable woodworking talents. Up here, in this delightful cozy room, this furniture looked nothing like the shabby, nicked up pieces of junk they were when her mother dragged them home from a flea-market.

On top of the glass-fronted bookcase, which was rarely opened, a mass of antique dolls huddled together for protection from the rougher toys and games that dominated the room, even though they remained hidden to the casual observer. But if all of her drawers and closet doors had suddenly sprung open, a person would see haphazardly constructed wooden model ships, puzzles, an erector set partially fashioned into some shape or other, binoculars, a flashlight, tennis racquets, lacrosse and field hockey sticks, a worn soft-ball glove, a basketball, and a single neglected video game lying in a corner of the armoire.

Spread out on a low table between the dormer windows was a 3-D puzzle of a house. This was Pam's current "thing"–building model houses. Right now, they were only 3-D puzzles, but she hoped that soon she'd get one of those big model house kits which were made out of real wood and that you put together with real nails and then painted with real grown-up paint. They were expensive, maybe even more than a bike. But with the money she'd earn this summer, who knows? She might even be able to get one of those, too. She thought about how nice it would be during the school year to come home to a project like that, es-pecially on those blustery cold, bleak winter evenings that were the off-season "treat" of living at the shore.

She plopped down in her rocker with a smile of satisfaction spread across her face. But she was no sooner comfortably seated, when something suddenly spurred her to leap up again, and race out the door.

As soon as she had reached the second floor, she knew she had gotten it right. Her mother was baking.

The scent of baked apples was starting to fill the whole house. As she burst into the kitchen, she saw that her mother was making one of her favorites, applesauce cake with raisins.

Mrs. Fischer looked up. "I saved you a piece of something new that I've made," she said as she handed Pam a lemon bar heavily dusted with powdered sugar. "Tell me what you think."

Pam eagerly bit into it, and then grimaced.

"That bad?" her mother exclaimed with surprise.

Pam doubled over with giggles. "No, no, it's not," she said, giggling with her mouth full. "It's just so *lemony*!"

"Well, it's a *lemon* bar, you knuckle-head!"

"I *know*, but I was hoping for something *applely*," Pam explained, polishing off the last bit and looking around for more.

"Wipe that powdered sugar off your face. I'm try-ing some new things for our Sunday morning brunch," her mother said. "Here, make yourself useful. Grease this muffin tin."

"Oooh! Giant muffins! Chocolate chip?" Pam asked hopefully.

"We'll see."

"We'll see, we'll see," Pam repeated, starting in on the pan. "It's always *we'll see*. Can't parents ever just say *yes* or *no?*"

"Be quiet, or you'll never see another muffin again, chocolate chip or otherwise."

Pam set to greasing the pan without another word. Every Sunday morning in the summer, as long as there were paying guests in the house, Sunday brunch was a big deal. Pam's mother and father prepared a massive amount of food, from fancy omelets and breakfast meats, to muffins and pastries. They set it all up in the formal dining room on a long table, with silver, crystal, and their best china. The guests would help themselves, and then take their plates heaped with food either to the living room or to the front porch, where there would be little tables and chairs set up for just this purpose.

"Make it special, and they'll keep coming back," was her father's motto, so her parents spent a lot of time cooking and trying out recipes. Next year they were determined to add afternoon tea, although neither of them could see how they would fit it all in.

"Well, *maybe*," Pam's mother would often say, when she and her husband would have these conversations, "if we had someone in to help who was a little more 'with it' we would have time for additional perks. As it is, our 'housekeeper' seems to have been hit on the head one too many times with a surfboard."

At this, Mr. Fischer would grin indulgently. "Ahh, he's just a harmless kid."

"I know, I know. That's the problem," Mrs. Fischer would retort.

Her parents had this conversation concerning Mike all through the winter, but come spring, Mike would once again be installed as the housekeeper/handyman.

As she greased the muffin tins, Pam talked about her new "job." She explained everything that Bob had told her she would be doing, especially the part about being the store's advertising.

"Sounds great. Just make sure you don't eat up all of their profits," her mother warned.

Pam giggled. "Naw. Hey, what's going in those?" she asked as her mother handed her two loaf pans.

"Pumpkin and zucchini bread."

Pam's mouth started to water. Thank goodness it was almost lunch time.

"And remember," her mother said, suddenly recalling something to mind, "tomorrow the new guests are coming to stay in the little house. They have a daughter your age, and I want you to be nice to her. Take her around town, or to the beach or something."

If anything could have burst the bubble of Pam's exuberant optimism, it was the prospect of having some hideous girl intrude on her summer plans. These plans consisted, aside from the time that she spent doing chores, and the time she was now going to spend at *The Chocolate Pot*, of doing what she pleased, whenever she wanted to do it.

Pam hated making friends. She tolerated her buddies at school because without them there'd be no softball, basketball, hockey, or lacrosse. But that didn't mean that she wanted them around all the time, and certainly not at home. There, they would be intruders, and she had enough of those with the inn guests all summer. Friends, except on the sports field, never wanted to do what she wanted to do, like explore the nature trail, or climb all the way up to the top of the lighthouse at Cape May Point, binoculars in hand. Especially girls. Girls never wanted to do fun stuff like that. All they ever wanted to do was sit around and talk.

And if there was anything Pam hated, it was sitting around, talking.

Pam looked outside the back door to the tiny Victorian cottage in the backyard. It was all the way at the back of the yard, and as small as a car garage. In fact, her parents had debated whether to build a garage for their beat up truck or a small guest house for people who wanted to rent a place at the shore for a whole summer. The guest house won, because they knew it would bring in more income, but they'd had to spend all their money last fall just to get it done. Consequently, they were a bit poor that year, which was why Pam's parents couldn't even think about replacing her bike.

The cottage was an exact replica of all the other Victorian houses in Cape May, right down to its gingerbread trim. It even had a tiny porch. This was the first summer it would be rented out, and Pam knew how important that was to her parents. But still, it just meant more intruders.

Pam licked the spoon loaded with batter for the zillionth time.

"Pam! Will you stop!" her mother cried in exasperation. "At this rate you'll have a whole loaf of zucchini bread in your stomach. Cut it out!"

Pam laughed. She then blew out her stomach as big as she could, and wobbled around the room as if a giant loaf of bread were blowing up inside her.

"Pam. Either help, or go to the beach."

Suddenly Pam stopped and her stomach shrank back to its normal size. "You know what?"

"What?"

"I forgot to ask them what I should wear. I mean, I don't even know if I have to wear a uniform."

Her mother shifted things around in the oven, and closed the oven door. The kitchen was getting hot.

"Just wear a nice shorts set. I think I've seen Katy wearing a brown apron when I've passed by the shop. You'll probably just slip it on over your outfit. And remember," her mother said to her, looking at her seriously, "don't eat too many of your fudge samples. It's a *job*," she pronounced emphatically, shaking her finger.

Pam giggled, and blew out her stomach again. "Yeah, I'd better not. Or else by the end of summer I'll look like *this*."

Mrs. Fischer sighed as Pam stumbled out of the kitchen, knocking into walls as if she were an enormous round ball.

Chapter Three

The next morning, Pam woke up to a beautiful sunny day feeling absolutely miserable, as if she'd had the worst nightmare. She stretched and rubbed her eyes, took in her bright, sunny surroundings, and then lay back against her pillow, as if it would make her feel better. Or at least remember what the trouble was.

Then suddenly she sat bolt upright. She did remember, alright. It was *The Chocolate Pot* that was the trouble. It was *The Chocolate Pot* that was making her feel sick. With a groan, she lay back again, and rolled onto her side thinking about her very first night of work—the very worst night of her life.

She had gone to the candy shop a little early, just as she'd been instructed. As she had made her way up to the boardwalk, her thoughts were full of bikes and model houses, along with an assortment of other things her new earnings would purchase, like the occasional soda or ice cream cone after one of her exploring expeditions. No longer would she have to rely solely on her allowance, scrimping and scraping to make it last through the week. Her pocket money was going to positively weigh her down!

The thought made her giddy. She imagined herself in shorts, loaded down with coins, lumbering along the boardwalk, heavily burdened with wealth. She would be so rich, in fact, that as she walked, she would hardly be able to lift her legs. She'd have to walk bow-legged, like a cowboy, with her thigh muscles straining with every step. She giggled to herself at the thought, and hurried on, oblivious to the strange looks that people were giving her as they strolled past her on the boardwalk.

She arrived at the shop, and entered, looking around for Bob's friendly face. But the only thing she saw was a group of tourists huddled around a display. At the sound of candies being poured into a bag, Pam realized that someone was behind the counter, even though she couldn't see who it was.

"Hello!" she called out.

The tourists turned around to look at her. Since no one else greeted her or said anything, she just stood there, looking embarrassed.

Then she saw an opening between two display cases, and decided that the best way to get noticed was to stand there. She edged between the two large, wooden cases and, behind them, saw the old woman who had been at the store the day before. Pam's heart sank.

As she just stood there, wondering how to get the

old woman's attention, the tourists paid for their pur-
chases, and left. The old woman then turned abruptly
around, and said sharply, "Well what are ya' standin'
there for? Let's go!"

Pam's mouth dropped open. "What?"

"Come on, let's go! You're not gettin' paid to stand
around gawkin'. Over here. Chop up this fudge, put
it on the tray, and get outside!" As she spoke, the old
woman waved her arm in the general direction of the
things she wanted Pam to do, but Pam was still completely at sea, and just stood there with her mouth
open.

"And get an apron on!" was the old woman's last
instruction, before she turned to a customer who had
just walked in.

Pam saw a row of aprons hanging on hooks toward
the back of the store. She walked over to them, and
reached up for the apron nearest her. She could hardly
see through the film of tears that had suddenly welled
up in her eyes.

As she adjusted the apron, which seemed about
ten sizes too big, she nervously tried to remember the
old woman's instructions. Something about a knife.
Well, there was a knife on the counter, a small one like
the ones her mother used for paring fruit. Pam picked
it up, and tried to remember what she was supposed
to do with it. The old woman had her back to her, so

Pam stood there for a second, looking around, trying to remember what she was there to do.

Fudge. Giving out fudge. Oh, yeah, she thought. I have to cut up fudge so I can give it out to people in small bites. But where was it?

Pam looked around in a state of confusion, wondering where they had hid the fudge. She was sure it was in the case, but where? She tried to remember what it was like when she had come in here as a customer, long before she had been inspired by this crazy idea to trade places with Katy for the summer. She thought about the cases, and how they had always looked, and remembered that the fudge was all the way in the front, so that the tourists could see all the varieties. Pam stood on tip-toe, and craned her neck forward.

There it was. Right in what was now, to her, the back of the case. Pam looked over at the old woman, wondering if she dared ask her for help, and decided against it. She leaned forward, straining her arm up over the work counter, deep into the case. Her fingers just about reached the soft, chunky mounds. She got one between two fingers, and pulled it forward, and set it on the counter, relieved. She was just about ready to start cutting it up, when she heard the customer say, "Oh, and some fudge. I'll take a pound of fudge." At that, the old woman turned to move in her direction.

Pam panicked, but then tried to look calm and nonchalant, as if cutting up cubes of fudge were something she did twenty times a day.

"What are ya' usin' *that* knife for?" the old woman hissed quietly, slamming down another, larger knife on the counter. She turned to the customer, and, oozing sweetness and charm, said, "What kind would you like?"

Hearing the old woman address the customer like that brought a flush to Pam's cheek. Apparently the old biddy could actually be nice. It was only to her that she was so mean. Why? What had she done? The back of her throat started to smart, and her eyes once again began to well up. Pam turned away, and quickly wiped them with her apron.

Unfortunately, just as Pam turned back to the counter, the customer left the store, and now it was just the two of them. The old woman came over to scrutinize what she was doing.

When she saw the result of Pam's nervous labor, she practically bellowed. "Wha'd'ya' think we're doin' here, workin' for free?" the old woman screeched at the top of her lungs. "Smaller, smaller, for cryin' out loud!!!" and she turned away.

Pam had no choice. She stuck her tongue out at the receding white head as far as it would go. Then she turned back to her work feeling slightly better.

Who was she? Pam wondered to herself. Bob hadn't even introduced her, so she didn't even know the old woman's name. She must be a relative, Pam thought. A *witch* relative.

She concentrated on cutting the pieces as small as she could. Soon a nice mound of tiny fudge chunks lay in a pile on the counter behind the tall glass cases.

Someone called over the top of the cases from the other side. "Could you help me please?" Pam looked up and momentarily panicked.

"Uh, um, uh, . . ." she began.

"I'll help ya', I'll help ya.'" The old lady waddled forward, remarkably fast for her age. She glared at Pam, and hissed quietly, "What are ya' waitin' for? Don' jus' stand around. Get a tray and get out there." She then turned to the customer and again oozed sweetly, her face crinkled up in smiles, "May I help you?"

Pam frantically looked around for a tray. There were piles of them everywhere, but she didn't know which one to choose. In a panic, she finally chose a medium sized aluminum tray that looked big enough for a small pizza. She looked at it doubtfully, and paused.

"Not that one!!" came hissing sharply in her ear.

Pam dropped the tray. She picked it up, and started to put it back on the counter.

"In the *dish room*. In the *dish room*!" the old lady barked.

Eventually Pam managed to get a tray, and a doily, and put all of the fudge cubes on it, all the while holding back stinging tears. She couldn't wait to go home.

As she started toward the door, the old woman barked one more order.

"And don't let all the kids stand around, eatin' the fudge and yammerin'!"

Pam closed the door behind her in relief.

"Phew!" She stood there for a second, just trying to calm down. At this point, she wasn't even sure a new bike was worth it. She wanted to go home, and she wanted to go home immediately.

Pam looked down at her enticing mound of fudge. At this point it looked like her only consolation. She thought of her mother's warning that she'd better not eat up all the fudge, and hesitated. Yeah, but these are battle conditions, Pam concluded to herself. Even mom would understand. And with that, she looked left and right, up and down the boardwalk, and then popped a chocolate cube into her mouth. As the fudge melted slowly over her tongue, a grin of satisfaction stole over Pam's face. This was her reward, and it was also her revenge. Maybe she would eat the whole tray after all. That would serve the old witch right.

For the first hour it was so slow, that to relieve her boredom, Pam played a game where for every ten people who walked by, she would pop another cube into her mouth, gradually trying the entire spectrum of flavors. Her legs began to ache, and so she shifted from one foot to the other, by now forgetting entirely the purpose behind standing there at all. Not one customer had even ventured in the direction of the shop the entire time. It was so boring, that she began to think that the only thing worse than standing there holding a tray watching people pass by, would be working inside with the ogre. Pam shuddered at the thought, and popped more fudge into her mouth.

Although the boardwalk had very few shops, *The Chocolate Pot* was definitely in the center of things. But it was still the dinner hour, and that meant that people were still eating in restaurants which were spread out over the whole of Cape May. It would be a while yet before they ventured up to the boardwalk to walk off their heavy dinners in order to fill up again on dessert.

Pam was dazing off into space, a lump of fudge--this time vanilla--gradually melting down in her mouth. She was so lost in a daze, that when the door of the shop opened abruptly, she jumped, nearly tossing the tray.

"Why don't ya' try sayin' somethin'," a voice rasped angrily.

"Huh?"

"Sayin' somethin'. What, are ya' deaf? Like, 'Hey, get some fudge at *The Chocolate Pot, The Chocolate Pot!*', the old woman yelled in an embarrassingly loud voice. Pam reddened as people looked their way. And just as abruptly, the door slammed shut.

Pam shook her head in disbelief. "*Witch*!"

She looked around, trying to muster up the courage to get the words out.

"Get some chocolate," she began, half out loud, half to herself, too embarrassed to get any louder. "I mean, fudge, fudge at the Pot, I mean *The Chocolate Pot*. . ." she sputtered, coming to a halt as people actually looked her way. She wanted to run inside and hide, but what lay behind that door was so much worse, she stayed put.

This was going to be a long night.

Chapter Four

As Pam sat there in bed, mulling over the events of the previous evening, the smell of bacon wafted into her room. With it came the sweeter scent of fresh muffins. Pam was up in a flash. She hurriedly grabbed her robe and slippers, and sped out the bedroom door. Nothing in the whole world would make her feel better than the breakfast that was waiting for her downstairs.

The hallway on the second floor was relatively empty of guests. Thank goodness!! No need to respond to the well-meaning, but annoying greetings of intruders. They were probably all at the breakfast buffet anyway, Pam thought as she hurried toward the kitchen.

And sure enough, as Pam settled in at the big round table that sat in the bay window of the kitchen, she could hear the sounds of the guests as they filled their plates, and then settled down to eat somewhere in the house or on the porch. Although there were only five guestrooms, when the house was full, it seemed like a throng of people inhabited it.

Her mother rushed through the swing door with a

plate and set it before Pam who was the only one at the kitchen table. Her parents both had their hands full every summer morning. Although it wasn't as elaborate as their Sunday brunch, every morning they cooked a complete breakfast for whoever had stayed at the inn the night before and then cleaned up after everyone was finished. It was quite a production, and kept her parents busy for hours.

Luckily, Pam had described her first night of work as soon as she had gotten home, running into the kitchen desperate to tell her parents how horrible it was, hoping that they would insist that she quit immediately.

Unfortunately, after acting out the things the mean old witch yelled at her, her father threw his head back and laughed. Pam started to protest, but her father broke in.

"Now Pam, you don't expect us to believe that this little old lady at *The Chocolate Pot* was that mean to you out of the blue, do you?" her father asked, chuckling. "Maybe what you're learning is that taking orders from a complete stranger is very different from taking orders from your parents. What you think is meanness, is probably something else."

"But she *was* mean. She *was*. She yelled at me *constantly*! And for no reason!" Pam burst into tears. "How come you don't believe me?"

Her father's eyes twinkled, as her mother reassured

her. "We do believe that you had a bad time, it's just that we think you may simply see things as worse than they are for a number of reasons."

"Such as?"

"Well, this was your very first time at a job, working with a grown-up who was a stranger. You were nervous, and you probably interpreted everything negatively because of that."

"*No*," Pam insisted. "I'm describing it just as it *was*. Horrible. Can't I quit?" she begged half-heartedly, knowing in advance what the answer would be.

Her mother looked at her father, but her father, eyes still twinkling, looked steadily at Pam. "No," he said quietly. "You have an agreement with your friend." Pam swallowed hard, feeling as if she were being punished. She just couldn't believe how bad everything was. She had gone off to bed frustrated at not being believed, and upset that, since Katy wasn't allowed a cell phone at camp, she couldn't call her to talk it over, or at the very least, find out who that hideous old witch was. Not that it would really make much of a difference. Because unless she suddenly caught a case of summer flu, she was going to have to face that hideous old witch again. Night after night.

But, even as Pam thought about all this, as she looked at the plate her mother had set in front of her, her depressed spirits began to revive. She picked up her fork, about to dig in, when her mother poked her head back into the kitchen.

"And don't forget. Today you're going to meet the little girl who's coming to stay in the cottage this summer. After your chores, don't disappear," her mother warned. She was off through the swing doors into the dining room.

Pam groaned, banging her forehead down onto the table nearly upsetting her plate. As if things weren't bad enough.

"Pa-aam!" Her mother's voice floated up to the third floor.

"O-*kay*!" Pam scrambled up from the 3-D puzzle she had been working on, and met her mother on the second floor landing.

"She's in the living room. *Be nice*," her mother ordered.

As Pam pretended to wilt like a drooping flower, her mom made a playful swat in the direction of her backside, which the little girl skillfully dodged. "That's for being so darned difficult!" her mother scolded.

She was referring to Pam's reaction to her initial suggestion that she simply send the girl on upstairs to her bedroom when she arrived.

"No *way*!" Pam had exploded, positively aghast.

"No intruders in my room!"

"In*truders?*" Mrs. Fischer had said, a little annoyed. "Remember, Pam, our guests are our bread and butter. *All* of them. Bread *and* butter!"

Pam now headed toward the living-room to meet the "bread and butter" feeling utterly put upon. She paused in the doorway, extremely uncomfortable with the idea of having to be friendly with a complete stranger.

As she hesitated, she noticed that the girl had her back to the doorway, giving Pam a chance to observe her.

She was taller than Pam, and although she wasn't *really* chubby, she gave the appearance of being so because her stomach stuck out like a toddler's. One of the girl's arms was twisted behind her back, clasping the other arm by the elbow. Her feet were spread out like a duck's, and overall, she gave the appearance of being just as nervous as Pam was.

Pam's greeting was stuck to the back of her throat.

"Hi. I'm Pam," she finally mumbled unenthusiastically, looking straight down at her feet.

The girl spun around and almost fell over as she unclasped her arms. She had a face full of freckles, with plump cheeks rounded out into a big smile. In fact, her whole face seemed to be caught up in the act of smiling. It was the most expressive face Pam had ever seen.

Simply in the course of untangling herself from her own arms and greeting Pam, she went through about ten different expressions.

"Gosh! Pam! You have a *fabulous* house!" The girl rapidly nodded her head up and down as she spoke, her eyes excited and friendly. "I mean *fab*-ulous! It's bea-oootiful! I'm Maddy!" She stuck out her hand, her head still bobbing up and down for emphasis.

Pam shook the other girl's hand, her eyes widened in amazement.

"This room is extraordinary! And the garden! I love gardens!" she said breathlessly as she floated toward a window, clasping her hands to her chest dramatically. "We have one at home, but it's not as nice as yours," she added in a sad tone, head bobbing some more.

Pam just looked at the girl. *This* was what she was going to have to spend her summer with? Suddenly, she wasn't sure which would be worse, days spent with this strange girl, or evenings being hounded by that mean old witch at *The Chocolate Pot*.

Remembering her manners, Pam asked the girl if she would like to be shown around.

"Oh, *yes*!" Maddy said excitedly, in a great big rush of air, almost knocking over an end table.

Without much enthusiasm, Pam began her tour of her house.

The Fischers had restored a rather large Victorian

house in the seaside town of Cape May, New Jersey, and transformed it into a successful bed-and-breakfast. The interior of the house was made to look just like a proper, elegant Victorian home. This meant that everything looked rather grand and expensive. And it *was* impressive on first sight.

Pam started her tour in exactly the same way her father did, every Friday afternoon when the Fischers opened the house to any tourists who wanted to see inside a real Victorian house. Her father always gave the tour, and by now, Pam knew it by heart.

"This room was built in. . .This room was originally used for. . .In the old days, they put their. . .over here you can see. . ." Pam droned on mechanically, in perfect imitation of her father. Maddy followed along patiently, "oooing" and "ahhing" at all the right places, her head nodding continuously throughout.

Suddenly, Pam stopped in front of a richly upholstered chair. "Do you believe my mom got this for thirty dollars at a garage sale? It was all messed up when she got it, and now look at it!"

"No! Wow!" Maddy exclaimed. "It's beautiful," she gushed. "How did she fix it?"

"I don't know, *exactly*," Pam said, shrugging her shoulders, suddenly wondering if she should be giving away the family secrets. Still, Pam was extremely proud of her parents' skills at restoration, and it was hard not to show them off. And Maddy was definitely a good audience.

"And this." Pam pointed to a richly carved mantlepiece. "My Dad found this at a flea market for twenty-five dollars!"

"Wow!"

"Yeah. Their workshop is in the basement. That's where they fix things up. Our motto is 'Junk goes in, furniture comes out!' And it's true! *This*," Pam said proudly, pointing to an end table, "my mom found in the trash, do you believe it? The *trash*!"

To Pam's satisfaction, Maddy appeared to be quite impressed as she gazed admiringly at a gleaming, perfectly polished wood table.

So the house tour continued, although now it was a bit different from the one her father gave on Friday afternoons. Fairly soon, the two were getting along fine. Maddy was a bit strange, but Pam decided that she was tolerable. So she suggested that they go to the beach.

"I'll have to check first with my mom," Maddy said, her head tilted to the side. "But I'm sure it'll be alright. I don't think she'll want me around while she's unpacking anyway. Besides, I have to get to the beach before Zara comes. She *hates* the beach."

"Zara?"

"My best friend. She's coming to stay this summer too. Then there'll be the three of us," Maddy said triumphantly, head bobbing in excitement at the thought.

Pam's heart sank in disbelief. *Another* one? *Another* intruder? When was it ever going to end?

Chapter Five

With their bathing suits underneath their shorts and tops, and with towels rolled up under their arms, the two girls made their way up the few blocks to the beach. The sun was hot, but a cool breeze rolled off the ocean. Seagulls squawked overhead. At the sound, Maddy looked up.

"I'm so happy! I'm so happy!" Maddy suddenly exclaimed, skipping along. "I missed the shore *so* much!"

Pam just looked at her.

"Of all the places we go, the shore is my ab-so-lute favorite!" Maddy's head bobbed violently with every syllable.

"Where else do you go?"

"Oh, Europe, and all," Maddy said with a wave of the hand.

Pam looked up at the boardwalk that ran along the beach front. In Cape May, nothing much was on the boardwalk, except in one spot, right where *The Chocolate Pot* was. Everywhere else it was empty. And it wasn't even made of boards. It was just a wide concrete slab that divided the road that ran beside it,

Beach Drive, from the sand dunes that rose up in uneven mounds on the other side. The dune grass was just visible from where they stood.

Pam tried to compare what she was seeing to what she knew of Europe.

"You mean Paris, and stuff?"

"Yeah. And London and Rome," Maddy added nonchalantly. She lifted her freckled face to the sun and took a deep breath of fresh, salty, sea air.

"I *love* the shore. You're so *lucky!*"

Pam wasn't feeling so lucky. She loved Cape May, but she didn't think it even remotely compared to Europe.

"So why did your parents rent a cottage in Cape May for the summer if you usually go to places like that?" Pam asked.

"My father is working on a case that he says will keep him in Philadelphia for several months. So we can't go anywhere far away right now. And my mom didn't want to travel with two kids anyway, *especially* Jimmy," Maddy said nodding, referring to her two-year-old brother. "Right now, he's a handful. So we came here so that Dad can just drive down whenever he can."

"So, what's your Dad, some kind of lawyer or something?"

"Uh huh."

The girls walked on in silence.

Pam suddenly felt weird and uncomfortable. She'd never been anywhere, not outside of New Jersey anyway. Her parents were always working, and for as long as she could remember, it had been at *The Sea Rose Inn*.

There was something else that was bothering her, too, in fact, weighing down on her like an overly huge dinner, something that she wanted to ask Maddy about. But Pam figured she'd wait to ask her till they had at least settled down on the sand.

The girls reached Beach drive, and stopped at the corner. Pam was looking down at the street, lost in thought. All of a sudden, a streak of green flashed by, causing her to quickly look up. Pam followed it with her eyes, her mouth gaping open in astonishment.

"What is it? What is it?" Maddy cried. "Why are you looking like that?"

Maddy looked in the direction in which Pam was gazing, but the only thing she could see was a girl speeding down the street on a bike.

"That's my *bike*!!!!" Pam finally sputtered out at the top of her lungs. "*My bike*!!"

Pam plopped down right in the sand, and sat there with her arms wrapped around her knees, fuming. She stared straight ahead, far out over the ocean with such an angry look that Maddy decided to leave her alone. She had calmed Pam down enough to gather a few of the details of her bike's theft, but Pam had still raged across the street, up onto the boardwalk, and down the ramp, and across a large tract of sand to the spot she chose.

While Pam fumed, Maddy set about carefully laying out her towel. She then took off her shorts and top, folded them neatly, and put them off to one side. She then lay down, flat on her back, a look of extreme contentment on her face. The two girls couldn't have been in more opposite moods.

The hot afternoon sun bore down on them. The sound of waves splashing onto the shore, the cries of children playing, and the squawking of seagulls high overhead all blended together into one pleasing sound. Maddy looked like she was on the verge of falling asleep, when suddenly Pam jumped up.

"Dang!" She cried angrily.

"Now what?" Maddy asked yawning.

"It's the beach tag inspectors. Come on." She sharply motioned for Maddy to follow her, after having quickly doffed her shorts and top. She ran down to the water's edge, with Maddy trotting behind, bewildered.

The girls reached the water's edge. Maddy hesitated, but Pam kept going, running further in until she was able to plunge head-first into a foaming breaker.

The chill of June waters stung Maddy around the ankles, and as the water lapped at her legs, she screamed, "No way! It's *freezing*! Are you crazy?"

Pam shouted over her shoulder, "Come on! I'll explain later!" and she moved further out.

Maddy stared at Pam as she repeatedly dove into the icy water. She tentatively moved forward, but the water was so cold it stung. Just then, a larger wave came crashing into shore, splashing against Maddy's torso like a sudden shower of ice cubes. She screamed again.

But Pam was nowhere to be seen.

Maddy stood there in the freezing water, shivering, looking this way and that, but she just couldn't see the other girl. Her teeth were chattering uncontrollably, and she was clenching her shivering arms with white fingers. But just as she was about to yield to panic, Pam's head bobbed to the surface. Maddy yelled to her, but Pam seemed to ignore her. Then, another shower of ice cubes bore down on Maddy, this time with such force it knocked her off her feet. As she clumsily stood up again, sputtering and gasping, she screamed "Pam!" at the top of her lungs.

This time, Pam heard her. She swung her head around, just visible above the surface, and saw Maddy stomping angrily through the swirling surf toward the beach. Pam caught the next wave, and body-surfed right into Maddy's legs, knocking her over again.

"Stop it!" Maddy cried out angrily, getting up with difficulty as the strong tide pulled at her legs. "I'm freezing! Are you crazy? What did we do this for anyway?" she sputtered furiously.

Pam simply laughed. "Just dive in, and stay under. You won't feel a thing. We have to stay in anyway. The beach tag inspectors are right near our stuff," she said, nodding her head over in the direction of their towels. "See?"

Maddy looked in that direction, and sure enough, a pair of girls in navy blue shorts and white tee-shirts were hovering over their towels as if they were looking for something.

"So!" Maddy said through chattering teeth. "What do *they* want?"

"They want us to either show our beach tags, or buy some. If we don't, they kick us off the beach," Pam said nonchalantly, talking to Maddy at the level of her shins. "That's why we had to go in the water. To escape them."

Maddy stomped her feet angrily. "Why didn't you say something before? I could have brought money. Besides, how come you don't have any of these tags? You *live* here."

"Of *course* I have a beach tag," Pam said with impatience, "and we have plenty of tags back at the house for guests. But where's the fun in that?" And with that, she dunked her head once more into the water, missing the look on Maddy's face.

For a couple of seconds, it looked like Maddy had completely lost the power of speech. Finally, she sputtered out, "You're *crazy*!"

"Come on," Pam yelled, coming to surface, and finally standing up. "Another big wave's coming! Dive!"

Maddy looked at the gathering swell twenty feet away, and then turned and looked longingly at the beach. Even if she tried to run in to shore to escape the coming wave, she was still going to be hit with an icy spray as it crashed. She made a swift decision, and, turning back toward where she had last seen Pam, plunged in.

As Maddy resurfaced, she gasped triumphantly through chattering teeth, "I did it! I did it!"

"Boy, you sure don't swim much. That was the worst dive I ever saw."

"Oh yeah?"

"Yeah."

"Well," Maddy said, struggling through her shivers to think of something to retort. "I bet you can't ride horses, or jump them, or anything."

"So? Who cares?"

"Well, who cares about diving then?" Maddy responded through chattering teeth.

Just then a huge swell gathered momentum and was about to break near their heads. Both girls simply sank below the surface, letting the turbulence rush past overhead. When they surfaced, they were actually in agreement on something--they'd had enough. They waited impatiently for the beach tag inspectors to move on a bit further down the beach, and then ran eagerly back to their spot, both of them shaking with cold by now. Pam hurriedly opened up her towel, getting sand all over it, and lay down.

As the girls lay flat on their backs, basking in the sun's warmth, Maddy got Pam to elaborate on her bike situation. Although, to Pam's exasperation, Maddy couldn't completely understand why her parents just didn't buy her a new one, she did lend a sympathetic ear, especially when she described her first dreadful night at *The Chocolate Pot*. And when she imitated the old woman, Maddy's shrieks of laughter were sufficiently satisfying for Pam to think that this girl might not be so bad after all.

Suddenly, Pam remembered the thing that she had wanted to ask Maddy.

"Did you say something about having a friend coming to stay?"

"Yes!" Maddy said excitedly. "My best friend in the whole world is coming to stay right next door! Isn't that great? We'll have so much fun!"

"Next door? Next door where?" Pam broke in, frowning.

"Next door!" Maddy said with a giggle, looking at Pam's perplexed face. "In that big square house right next to yours."

Pam thought for a minute, trying to process what Maddy was saying. There was only one big square house next to theirs. "But that house is empty!" Pam exclaimed. "No one lives there!" And no one ever had, for as long as she could remember.

"Well," Maddy said gently, laying her head back down on her towel, "they do now."

Pam's face registered the full extent of her dismay and disappointment. She was just getting used to *this* girl, and now there'd be *another* one? Good grief, it was an invasion!

After a few minutes of silence, during which Pam tried to think, she burst out with, "I don't get it. How do *you* know? How did this happen? Isn't that some kind of weird coincidence?"

Maddy laughed, and then explained that her "best friend in the whole world" had a great-aunt and grand-mother who owned that house. When Maddy had found out during the school year that Zara was going to be staying with them for the whole summer in Cape May, she begged her mom to find a place as close by as possible. And she did! Right next door.

"Zara?"

"Yes. That's my best friend's name. Isn't it great? Anyway, you'll *love* her!" Maddy gushed, her head nodding against the sand.

"Oh, *brother*."

The girls were silent for a while, the one resting contentedly with a slight smile on her face, the other scowling upwards at the sun. This time, Maddy broke the silence.

"Hey, I have an idea."

What now, Pam thought with irritation.

"Why don't you just get back the bike you had? It would be so much easier than putting up with that horrible old lady. Even if you do get to eat all the candy you can sneak."

"Fudge."

"Whatever. But still. Just get back the bike you had. It's yours, after all."

Pam turned her head and looked at Maddy in disbelief. "Are you *nuts*? Do you mean *steal* it back?"

"Well, not *steal* it, exactly, but maybe you could track her down, you know, like a detective, and confront her, and, and. . ." Maddy ran out of ideas as to what would follow.

"And just ask her to give it back. Just like that. Maybe tell her the whole sob story of my job and all, so maybe she'll feel sorry for me and give me back the bike that she crept up onto my property and stole from my house in the first place. Good grief!"

"Well, it was just an idea," Maddy said defensively.

A *dumb* idea, Pam thought to herself. A dumb, dumb, dumb idea. Now she was really irritated. She looked over at Maddy nestled peacefully on her towel, face turned up to the sun, seemingly about to drift off.

"Don't fall asleep," Pam said.

"Hm?" Maddy said, drowsily.

"Don't fall asleep. We may have to make another run for it."

"What!!" Maddy cried, lifting her head up off the towel.

"Yeah. The inspectors. You don't think that they just come through one time, and that's it, do ya?"

As Maddy let out a moan of dismay, Pam continued cheerfully.

"Oh, no. We'll be running back and forth all afternoon." At that, Pam settled down onto her towel, a grin spread across her face.

Chapter Six

Pam still did not know the name of the mean old lady at *The Chocolate Pot*, nor who she was. Every time she would work up the courage to approach her, the old lady would brush her off, and busy herself with some task. It was almost as if she were doing it on purpose. Worse, Katy's father was now away, tending to another of their family's stores whose manager had gotten sick. So here, the old woman was actually left in charge. Pam felt sick at the thought.

She shifted from one leg to the other, bored stiff even though it was only 6:15. Only one hour and forty-five minutes to go. She shifted the tray from one arm to the other, using the other hand to steady it. Her eyes wandered up and down the boardwalk.

It wasn't the traditional wooden boardwalk found at most New Jersey resorts except for the area where Pam was, which had a small number of T-shirt shops, a couple of candy and ice cream stores, and even a small arcade. The remaining all-concrete walkway, which stretched for a mile and a half in each direction, was usually populated in the mornings by tourists walking, riding bikes, or jogging. But in the evening, after gorging all day and then topping it all off with a huge dinner as if they hadn't seen food in weeks, most people just waddled along the walkway, stomachs stuck way out in front, heads turning this way and that, looking for that last bedtime morsel to cram in–candy or ice cream, or both.

The Chocolate Pot was in the middle of this small center of activity, but now, there was no activity whatsoever, not even from the hungriest tourists. Pam considered this with some concern, thinking that if she didn't drum up business soon, the old biddy would be out the door barking at her.

Pam turned around and looked in the window, into the shop. It was nearly empty, which meant there was nothing to distract her from hounding Pam. The knot of anxiety in her stomach increased.

She looked down at her tray at the heap of fudge cubes. She had cut all kinds tonight. Fudge-nut. Strawberry. Vanilla. Chocolate. Chocolate with marshmallows. And mint chip. That was her favorite. It was green, after all.

She decided to pop one of those into her mouth after making sure no one was looking. Hm. It was pretty good. In fact, too good for tourists. She shifted her tray around so that the mint chip cubes were at the back, nearest her, and hardest for tourist fingers to reach. If

I play this right, she thought to herself, I'll be able to keep all these for myself.

As the fudge cube melted in her mouth, she thought about this past week, and what it was like spending time with Maddy. She had decided that Maddy wasn't too horrible after all, but when she thought about the impending invasion of Maddy's friend Zara, she felt considerably annoyed. After all, it was one thing to be forced to tolerate one intruder, but it was entirely another to have to put up with the intruder's "best friend in the whole world."

Pam thought about how Maddy described her friend, as a second cube came to rest on her tongue.

Apparently, she took ballet lessons, a lot of them, and very seriously. She did Cotillion also, but less often and less seriously. (Whatever that was.) She took piano, but preferred drawing. She read books constantly, and not just kid books. For fun, she went shopping, but only bought the best designer clothes. (Naturally.) At one point in this recital of her talents, Pam interjected "Are you sure she's *eleven?*" but then, to her chagrin, Maddy enthusiastically corrected her, her head bobbing, "No, she's ten. She skipped a grade."

Apparently, the only flaw this rich, cultured, well-traveled ten year old had was that she couldn't ride horses. ("She's allergic to them, or something. . .") And, according to Maddy, for a while there was a scare that she'd already developed an eating dis-order, because once, when their school went away to camp, she didn't eat the entire three days. "*Three whole days*!!" Maddy exclaimed, still in disbelief.

"So, what was her problem?" Pam had asked, not really giving a hoot, and even further dreading the ar-rival of this creature.

"Oh, well, she didn't tell anyone at the time, but she just couldn't stand the food. I mean, her family has a chef who cooks for them at home, and even I have to admit the camp food was pretty bad."

"A chef?? At home?? Every *day*?? Oh, *brother*!"

As Maddy continued to brag about her friend's ac-complishments during the course of the week, Pam couldn't help wondering what Miss Perfect saw in Maddy, who, though extremely good natured, was not exactly "perfect" material. Her stomach stuck way out, and when she walked, she sort of waddled. And although she was hardly hideous or anything, her freckles did seem to have taken over her face. To be honest, Maddy was more like a boisterous puppy than a Miss Perfect, and that was rather nice. But Pam couldn't understand how these two got along, if they were as different as she imagined them to be.

It was starting to get a bit more crowded on the boardwalk, so Pam decided to take a temporary break from sneaking fudge. Nothing was more embarrassing than having a tourist catch her in the act, and worse, tease her about it.

"Hey, can I have one of those?" A big, burly man reached for the tray.

"Er, sure," Pam said awkwardly. She knew she should be more encouraging, but the words just wouldn't come up out of her throat.

"Well now, *that* sure is a nice job." The man's wife came up to join her husband, and also reached for the tray. "If I were you, I'd be snacking on these all night," she said to Pam, winking.

Pam's only response was to mumble awkwardly, and look down at her feet. The couple walked away without going into the store.

As if right on cue, the shop door exploded open.

"You call that SELLIN'???" the old lady shrieked. "I could sell shoe shellac better!! *Say* somethin' next time!!"

The door slammed closed.

Pam wiped small beads of sweat from her brow, beads which appeared every time that woman so much as looked in her direction. As a reward for surviving the storm, Pam threw caution to the wind and treated herself to another cube.

"Ha! I saw that!" A tourist bore down on her with a conspiratorial grin. "You better watch it. You don't want one of these." The man patted his big round belly and walked on. Pam squirmed in embarrassment.

The sun was just beginning to drop down behind the Victorian houses that lined the opposite side of the street, and so Pam could now look around without squinting in the glare of the setting sun. As she did, something suddenly caught her eye.

Across the boardwalk, right next to where concrete steps went down to the street, was a bike rack. It stood at street level, so from where Pam was standing, only the very tops of the bikes were visible. But she was certain of one thing: that yellow basket was familiar. If only she could get a little closer to take a better look.

She turned around to look in the store. The old woman and two other employees were busy talking. Pam looked up and down the boardwalk. She felt funny even thinking about moving out of her spot—it would be like going off the job. But she just *had* to take a closer look.

Pam looked around once more, for what, she wasn't quite sure, for there were more tourists now, than earlier. Then she moved tentatively forward, dodging people walking in either direction. At the edge of the boardwalk she stopped, and looked directly down at the bike rack.

A bike, whose glistening green paint was a bit

worn, rested on the rack directly below her. In a daze of disbelief, she looked at the yellow basket decorated with the pink flowers that she had hated when she had first gotten the bike home. Now she looked at them like they were long lost friends. Pam experienced a weird twinge of pain and bewilderment as she stared at something that was hers, but not hers.

She looked around, wishing someone could give her an idea of what to do. But all those strangers passing to and fro were no help. After all, what would she say?

She looked back down at the bike. It was as if she knew it as a friend, and she was sure it knew her too, and wanted rescuing. But it was secured to the bike rack with a lock, and not a flimsy one either.

Frustrated, and with tears stinging her eyes, Pam knew that the only thing was to get back in place before the old biddy came storming out again.

Back in her spot, her tray seemed to invite a swarm of samplers, some of whom were actually going into the store to buy some fudge, but only after discussing the merits of each type in excruciating detail. Pam just wanted them all to go away, so she could think about what to do. She answered questions mechanically while she tried to form a plan of action. She wanted desperately to call her parents and ask them what to do, but at the moment, that was out of the question.

Then she thought of something that calmed her down at first, but brought with it a different, new kind of uneasiness. At least I'm *standing* here, and I'll be able to see who comes to collect it, she thought. But she felt queasy at the idea of actually seeing the bicycle thief up close.

Pam went into the shop to reload her tray. When she came back out, she fixed her gaze on her bike, determined that nothing would distract her.

But the crowd had thickened around the shops, and at the same time, it was now twilight. Lights went up in store windows and the street lamps now shone on the boardwalk, making a very brightly lit spot in the middle of the gathering darkness. Now, she could only just make out the yellow basket.

Suddenly, a large group of people crowded around her, sampling from the tray and making small jokes, as if to cover their own embarrassment at having a piece. Pam's responses were automatic, and not very enthusiastic. She had heard these same jokes every night for a week now.

She could hardly contain her impatience for the crowd to move on, so that she could return to her watch. But just as soon as it looked as if she'd be able to see across the boardwalk once more to where the basket was dimly illuminated, another large group moved in, sampling, and gushing, and making the same jokes.

Finally, after about forty minutes of this, when her shift was nearly over, the crowd in front of her thinned, and she had a chance to look over to the bike rack once again.

It was gone.

She stared in disbelief. How could someone have come to retrieve the bike right in front of her without her seeing a thing? Tears of frustration welled up, and the back of her throat stung as more tears gained momentum. She drew her arm across her face, back and forth, so that no one would see her crying, absolutely miserable that her bike had been taken from her, again, only this time right before her very eyes.

Chapter Seven

"Here, you put the claw in the ground like *this*, push down with your left hand, and twist the handle with your right." Pam's mother was showing her how to aerate the soil. "Do you think you know how to do it? Do you think you *can* do it?"

"Yeah, I can do it," Pam said grumpily.

Her mother patted her on the head. "Thanks. If you need help, holler. I'll be up here with the roses."

Pam's mother walked to the front portion of the yard. Pam was all the way at the back, on one side of the house. She looked at the long stretch of flowers which were planted below a very tall hedge which marked the line of the property on one side. The hedge and the flowers ran the entire length of the property. There wasn't much space between the house and this hedge, just enough for the row of flowers, and a few feet of plush green grass in-between. Maybe it was a total of five feet wide. It was a nice space when it was done. It was the *doing* that was the problem.

Facing the front of the house, that border was on the right, and the driveway was on the left, on the side next to the big square mansion that was soon to be inhabited. Between the mansion and the Fischer's driveway grew a short hedge, and there, thought Pam with relief, was no room for any flowers, or anything at all that needed to be aerated, weeded, plucked, or primped. You could also see easily over the short hedge, which Pam thought her mother had ensured on purpose, because that property was so good to look at. Even if it did make Mrs. Fischer a bit jealous.

It was done in a far different style than the Fischer's inn. It was grand, with big beech trees lining the front, and various bushes spread out decoratively in the small front yard. The only spot of color sprang from stone urns placed on either side of wide wooden steps leading up to the massive wrap-around porch. This year, the urns held red geraniums, which spilled out abundantly. Pam's mother often whined, "No one even lives there, and their garden is better than ours!" which frustrated complaint usually resulted in Mrs. Fischer throwing herself even more energetically into her garden, which usually looked great except for one thing. The roses.

Ah, those roses. They bordered the front of their inn, just behind a low white picket fence, and they were Mrs. Fischer's pride and joy. The only problem was, they looked hideous. They were limp and sickly imitations of rose bushes, and nothing Pam's mother could do would coax them into better shape. They were so bad, that every summer Pam and her father begged her to replace them with something else–anything–just something that would look like normal plant life.

"But it's called the *Searose Inn*. How can a place called the *Searose* not have any roses?" she would wail in despair.

So each summer brought out in Mrs. Fischer a renewed zeal for coaxing them into life, but always to no avail. Lately, at the dinner table, Pam and her father had been tossing around possible alternate names for the inn.

Before long, it was positively scorching as the sun bore down on the yard. Pam tried to squeeze herself into the little patch of shade made by the tall hedge. She wiped her dripping brow with the back of her hand.

"Watcha doin'?" Maddy asked, as she came out of the little cottage and bounded across the short stretch of lawn toward Pam.

"Aerating the soil," Pam said, out of breath and not in the best of moods.

"What's that?"

Pam looked at her, too weary and hot to fully express her annoyance. "I'm making the hard, packed dirt around the plants loose and fluffy, see?" She pointed to the contrast between the area which she had completed, and the long stretch ahead of her yet. "Besides, how come you don't know that? I thought you had a garden."

"We do. But we have people come and do this stuff. Besides, they just put those brown wood chips and stuff around the plants."

"Mulch. It's called mulch. And when I'm done here I'll be putting that on top." Pam wiped her brow again.

"Isn't that usually done sooner? Like in April or May?" Maddy asked.

Pam thought to herself, yes, mulch is definitely put down sooner, but because my parents were too busy finishing your dumb cottage to plant in time I'm stuck doing it now, in this hot sun. She drove a claw into the ground and twisted hard.

"We're late this year," she said between clenched teeth.

"Oh. Can I do some?" Maddy asked, head bobbing enthusiastically.

Pam looked at her skeptically, and then drew a deep breath. "Mom, can you please get another claw thingy for Maddy?"

Once Maddy was equipped, Pam showed her what to do.

"You work about four feet ahead of me. I'll work toward you, then when I catch up, we'll switch places. Right?"

"Right," Maddy said with an emphatic nod.

Soon both girls were working steadily as they chatted, although Maddy did seem to pause a lot to stare off into space. Pam decided in no time that she was a pretty lousy helper. But then, it wasn't her garden, or her chore.

So she listened while Maddy chatted about her school, her hobbies, and Zara's impending visit, grunting now and again to show that she was listening. Eventually, having exhausted all of the topics she had for conversation, Maddy moved on to the subject of Pam's bike. A few days had passed since the night Pam had seen it parked on the bike rack, but her disappointment at having been so close to it while powerless to do anything still stung Pam. She explained to Maddy that even though her parents were upset over the bike's reappearance, there was nothing that they could do about it. Pam knew they were sympathetic, but she still wanted more. She wanted *action*. Maddy nodded her head in understanding.

"I mean, what can I *do?*" Pam asked forcefully, not really expecting an answer.

Maddy paused again, and picked dirt off of her gardening claw.

"I've got an idea!" she suddenly said excitedly. "Maybe I could go to work with you every night, and some night when the bike's there in the rack, I could stay, and sit there casually on a bench, pretending to be minding my own business, but all the while," she said, her eyes narrowing here and her head nodding with every syllable, "keeping a hawk's eye on the bike. Then, when the thief comes by to pick it up. . ." She reached a dramatic pitch, but not knowing exactly where to take the drama next, trailed off. "Hm." She slumped back down, and started to pick dirt off the claw again.

"Yeah? And then?"

"Well," Maddy said, shrugging her shoulders, "if I saw the person, at least we'd know who it was."

"I already know who it is. It's some girl with blond hair. We saw her that first day, remember?"

"Oh yeah." She shrugged her shoulders again, tilted her head to the side, and thought some more.

"Well, maybe when she comes up to the bike, I could give you a signal, and you could come rushing over, and we could both. . ."

"Yeah?" Pam pressed sarcastically. "Take her on? Beat her up? Steal the bike back? What?"

Maddy giggled at the scenario. Just then, Mike the handyman broke in. "Whoa, dudes, yur not talking about bashin' in heads, are ya? And stealin'? Two nice little girls like you? Whoa. What are things comin' to?"

The girls' heads swung round, to see Mike striding by, carrying a full can of paint.

"Hey, what are you listening in for?" Pam asked, annoyed.

"Dudes! I've got ears! I can't help hearing as I'm walkin' by with this paint. But dudes, it's not cool. Really it isn't. Don't go beatin' up other little girls. It's not nice!" And with these words of wisdom, Mike shook his head, and continued on, rounding the front of the house. Pam stared at the trail of paint-splattered grass that followed in his wake.

Maddy giggled again. "But seriously. We could confront her, you know, and ask her, like. . ."

"Why the heck did you steal my bike, and can I have it back now, please?"

"*Yes*," Maddy said with surprising force, and with another of her sharp nods of the head. "Yes, *exactly*."

"I was joking. Besides, what would be the point?"

"To have it out with her."

"That's stupid."

"Are you afraid?"

Pam nearly exploded. "*Afraid*? Are you *kidding* me?"

"I think you're afraid."

Pam shot Maddy a dirty look, and then sat and thought for a minute. She squirmed at the idea of being afraid, but she also knew that the idea of meeting up with that blond-haired girl didn't sit right with her. Was she afraid? How pathetic.

Pam haltingly began to speak. "I'm not afraid, *exactly*, but it is weird, you know, going up to someone who's done something bad to you, and, well. . ."

"Confronting them with it?" a voice asked far above them.

Both girls looked up. Mr. Fischer was leaning out of a window on the second floor. Pam reddened with embarrassment knowing that her father, too, had been listening in. "Yes, Pam. Confrontation is scary, even over things much more trivial than your bike theft. But I don't think that what you have in mind is a good idea. I definitely don't want you to get into a fight, or even an argument with this girl. I don't want to see you hurt any more than you already have been."

With that, Mr. Fischer pulled his head back in through the window.

Pam rolled over onto her side, pretending to be writhing in pain. "*Eavesdroppers!* I live in a household of eavesdroppers! Gagh!"

Maddy giggled again, but shrugged her shoulders as she looked up toward the second floor again. "I don't know. I think you're lucky to have your parents around all the time. I never see my Dad."

Pam remained on her side, groaning.

After a while, they resumed working, and quite a while later, a bit after midday and nearing lunchtime, they had actually finished the entire row. They both stood up, and looked at what they'd done. The narrow bed had been planted with yellow marigolds and pink petunias, alternating in large clusters all the way down the row. Now the dirt around the flowers looked all clean and fluffy, making the yellow and pink flowers stand out brightly against the dark background.

"Wow!" Maddy exclaimed. "It looks great! I can't believe we did all that! I never worked so hard in my whole life!"

Pam wiped her dripping brow with the back of her dirty hand, and gave Maddy a look.

"Never?"

"No. I never do chores," she said casually, shrugging her shoulders and grinning. "Not like you. You guys sure do work a lot around here."

Pam was still looking at Maddy in disbelief. "No chores? None? At all? Hey mom," Pam shouted over to her mother, "she doesn't do any chores!"

Her mother turned around from the rosebed, her face beaded with moisture. "Guess what? Too bad. You do." She turned back to the dirt and the sickly looking plant embedded in it. "Besides, when you're older, you'll thank me."

"Ugh! No way!" Pam slumped miserably down on the ground. Maddy just stood there looking cheerful and awkward at the same time.

"Besides," Mrs. Fischer continued, taking a look at her daughter, "don't you like making things beautiful?

Look at what you did today. That's beautiful, and *you* did it."

Pam stubbornly covered her eyes with her hands, and Maddy giggled. Her mother let out an exasperated sigh.

Just then, they all heard the sound of a car pulling into a driveway nearby. They turned to look, and saw a long, black Mercedes slowly creeping up the driveway of the big square house next door. The car looked totally out of place. No cars in Cape May were ever that new, that bright, and that expensive all at the same time. Pam got up from the ground to take a look, and even Mrs. Fischer and Mike, from their different places, stopped what they were doing.

Only Maddy wasn't standing stock still, staring. At first sight of the car pulling in next door, she had scampered away, down the Fischer's short drive, around the hedge, and up the drive on the other side. She was at the rear car door before it had even opened.

"Zara!" she cried, leaving the onlookers in no doubt as to who had finally arrived. Pam looked at her mom, said, "Oh, brother!" and rushed into the house before anyone could stop her.

Mike had resumed painting, but Mrs. Fischer couldn't resist staring at that shiny new car. Then, with a small sigh, she knelt back down, and resumed her work.

Chapter Eight

Six whole days passed before Pam (and her parents) got to satisfy their curiosity about their new neighbors. Mrs. Fischer kept looking over at the house with even more longing than before, and was beginning to bore her family at the breakfast table with her constant speculations on its interior. Pam didn't even see Maddy once during that entire time, and was torn between relief that silence finally reigned in her world, and annoyance that her new friend could drop her so abruptly. "Girls!" was all she'd say, with a shake of her head.

Of course, the Fischer's house was still a hub of activity, and would be until the end of August. That meant that Pam was constantly dodging both guests and her harried parents, who scurried around from morning to night, each and every day, each secretly wishing that September would hurry up and get there.

But Pam managed to escape the chaos of her crowded home, for she spent her mornings working in the peaceful yard and her days exploring Cape May as well as she could without a bike. Sometimes she met up with friends at the outdoor mall, and together they'd gorge themselves with as much ice cream as their allowances would permit, and then run up to the beach and throw themselves into the icy-cold surf—as soon as the beach-tag inspectors weren't looking, naturally. Everyday was happy and peaceful, at least until she had to face the ogre at *The Chocolate Pot*.

But it wasn't to last. On the morning of the seventh day, one full week after the Mercedes had pulled into the drive next door, a summons to tea was dropped through the slot in the front door. The invitation was for 3:00 that very afternoon, and Pam's mother was going to make sure that she looked sharp. Since that meant a reprieve from weeding for one morning ("You'll never get the dirt out from under your fingernails!") having to look sharp wasn't so bad.

So at precisely 3:00 in the afternoon, Pam, with shiny hair and clean fingernails, climbed the porch stairs of the house next door. She felt weird. She was so used to looking at this house as off-limits that she couldn't shake off the feeling of being a trespasser. And, she had to admit, she was nervous. This Zara character sounded like a piece of work. Not to mention that there was something so formal about the place. Even the invitation was formal. Whatever happened to Maddy just bouncing across the yard and into the house?

She turned her head, and looked over at her own house, which, intruders and all, looked so comforting just then. As she reluctantly raised her hand to press the doorbell, the door suddenly burst open.

"PAAAAAAAAM!!!!!" Maddy exuberantly shouted.

"Hello."

"PAAAAAAAAM!!!!!" Maddy cried again, as if Pam had just arrived safely--and unexpectedly--home from a far off expedition. "I'm so happy to see you! How've you been?" Maddy gushed. Then, not waiting for an answer, she enveloped Pam in a big bear hug.

Eventually, Pam managed to extricate herself, and was about to respond with a greeting of her own, when Maddy broke in.

"Come in, come in. Meet Zara and her Aunt Caroline!" Maddy bounced back into the house, and in through a doorway on the left side of the enormous entrance-hall, leaving Pam to gape at her surroundings.

The hall was twice as big as her own. It was so big, in fact, that except for the giant mahogany staircase rising up out of the floor like a fantastically ornate wooden sculpture, it could have been a living room in itself.

Pam recalled her mother's orders to keep her "eyes peeled," so she stood there for a minute, carefully taking note of her surroundings. After all, if she didn't have details for her mother, and lots of them, she'd never hear the end of it.

"Paaaam!" A voice called from the next room.

Pam turned toward the doorway, and entered the next room with a slight giggle and a mumbled "sorry." She found herself in a room unlike any that she had ever seen in Cape May. It was all bright and airy, with tall ceilings seeming to rise up forever, and with French doors at the front and sides that let long shafts of sunlight stream in. She'd seen a lot of Cape May houses since her mother dragged her around to every single one that was open to the public, but none of them were done in such light colors, or had painted (painted!) furniture. Pam just stared in awe at a room that looked fit for a queen, and suddenly felt unsure about the accuracy of her coming report to her mother. How on earth was she going to describe *this*?

As she stood stock still, gaping at all the finery, Maddy started to giggle. Pam looked at her, and then at the other two people in the room. Never had she seen two such completely different expressions looking back at her simultaneously.

One of these belonged to a little old lady with china blue eyes and pure white hair who was grinning in amusement. But she wasn't just grinning, she was twinkling, too, her eyes blinking rapidly, and her shoulders shrugging, as if a greeting weren't a proper greeting unless it was expressed in a series of joyful twitches.

The other expression belonged to a tiny, fragile-looking little girl whose face was so devoid of expression that she looked like a statue. Her extremely dark hair was pulled into a tight bun at the top of her head, and even though she was wearing jeans and a simple top, she still managed to look thoroughly prissy. Pam just stared at the girl, while the other girl returned her gaze, although just barely, for Zara looked in Pam's direction through large, cold brown eyes, as if determined to not actually see her, even though she was just five feet away.

Oh, brother, Pam thought to herself.

Maddy hurried through the introductions so that they could all get down to business at the table of goodies that had been set up in front of one of the tall windows. It was a scrumptious array! There were pink cupcakes with silver beaded sprinkles; there was a huge cake slathered in creamy vanilla icing and decorated with soft lavender petals; there were several dishes with tiny icinged squares that Pam learned were called *petits-fours*. It looked like a wedding feast with the pretty china cups, saucers, and plates, all set on a white lace tablecloth.

A maid in a uniform came in to help serve the tea and cakes, and before long, amid giggles from Maddy and Pam, complete silence from Zara, and many winks and blinks from the aunt, the sugary treats that had initially graced the table like delicate works of art were happily destroyed.

Maddy and Zara's aunt, who seemed to know each other quite well, launched into an animated discussion of the entire Harry Potter series. Pam's eyes widened at the idea of this little old lady reading kid books, but then it did seem to sort of fit. She listened with amazement to their discussion. They picked apart their favorite scenes, recalled exciting Quidditch matches, debated which Hogwarts teacher was the wackiest and which one was their favorite, and made predictions about what would happen in the last one. Pam, who wouldn't pick up a book unless her life depended on it, sat there dreading the inevitable moment when they'd ask her opinion. When the conversation paused, Pam decided to redirect it a little.

"Um. . .er. . .what should I call you?" Pam asked Zara's aunt through a mouthful of cake, Maddy having only introduced her as "Zara's aunt."

"Hm. . ." the old woman blinked up at the ceiling as if the answer were to be found hidden up there amidst the ornate plaster-work. "How about 'Aunt Caroline'?" she finally pronounced excitedly, with several winks, a grin, and a couple of shrugs of her shoulders.

At this, Zara somehow managed to look even stonier, prompting Pam to respond eagerly with "Thanks, Aunt Caroline!" before settling into another treat. So far, the other girl had yet to say one word. It was almost as if the others weren't even there, Pam thought with amazement. Zara's silence was especially strange in contrast to how animated Maddy and Aunt Caroline were. The two of them chatted up a storm as if there were no age difference at all between them, even though it had to be about sixty years.

Unfortunately for Pam, the conversation returned to the Potter books. She listened carefully and feigned interest by periodically nodding, even though she had no idea what they were talking about, while Zara continued to sit there, picking daintily at her cake, oblivious to them all.

Eventually, Maddy turned to Pam. "So, what do you think? Which Potter book was your favorite so far?"

Darn! The moment she'd been dreading. "Uhm. . .well. . ." Pam said thickly through a glob of cake, "I. . .uh. . .haven't read Harry Potter. . .*yet*," she confessed reluctantly.

Maddy's eyes bulged in surprise. "Whaaaat!" she screeched. "You haven't read Harry *Potter*? You're *kidding* me!" she shouted at the top of her lungs. Even Aunt Caroline looked surprised, her bright blue eyes now unblinking and as wide as saucers.

Pam swallowed hard, and said emphatically, "No, I haven't." And then, throwing caution to the wind, she added, "I *hate* reading!"

There was a shocked pause for a moment while everyone digested this strange admission. The silence was only broken by Zara snorting in disgust.

Maddy recovered first, and, noting Pam's reddened face, quickly plunged forward. "Huh. I can't believe I didn't know that. Well," she added with a laugh, "I guess that's why your books are always so neatly stacked in your bookcase. You never take them out! But still," she continued, tilting her head to the side and nodding vigorously, "you *should* at least read Harry Potter."

Pam shrugged. "Maybe. But I've got other stuff to do. Like going to the beach, and. . ." she almost said 'riding her bike' but added instead "and going around. . .and. . ." she trailed off, unable to put all that she did into words, but catching Zara's contemptuous sneer, she pounced on the last thing as if suddenly remembering it. "And my *job*! I've got my *job*!" She glared triumphantly back at Zara, daring her to top that, but the other girl had swiftly resumed her impassive expression.

"That's right," Maddy said enthusiastically, taking up Pam's cause. "Pam's got a job, a real job, where she gets paid and everything. And it's in a *candy* store," she added impressively, as if there were no finer credentials than that.

"Oooh!" Aunt Caroline exclaimed, full of excited winks and blinks. "Tell us about the *candy* shop!"

So, anxious to redeem herself, Pam launched into an account of her duties at *The Chocolate Pot*, and before long, had everyone except Zara in stitches over her description of the old grouch she worked with. To Aunt Caroline's delight, she even acted out the "old bulldog" barking orders at her, along with exaggerated imitations of how tourists would come up to her for "just a little bite" and then gobble up whole handfuls of fudge. At this, Aunt Caroline had tears in her eyes from laughing so hard, and since Maddy was practically on the floor, Pam, feeling immensely satisfied with herself as she calmly sat back in her chair, barely resisted the urge to stick out her tongue at the still unyielding Zara.

Pam finally asked to be excused to the bathroom, having suddenly remembered her mission. She was directed upstairs, and so made her way back into the hallway, and ascended the dark, massive staircase, which, to tell the truth, did not go with the light, airy feeling of the rest of the house. She made a mental note to tell her mother this.

On the wide landing, she caught a glimpse through open doors of other rooms. A lot of them were not furnished, which made sense as the house was rarely occupied. But Pam did take a lingering peek at the front bedroom which was not only furnished, but extravagantly so. It had sky blue walls with gleaming white trim. It had white and blue furniture, with glimpses of pink showing here and there. There were crystal vases scattered all over the room that sparkled in the afternoon light, and there was even a gigantic white chandelier that looked like it was made of china hanging impressively from the center of the ceiling. It was simply exquisite.

Boy, would my mom love to see this, Pam thought to herself as she stared. Then she realized that they must be wondering where she was, so she hurried up in the bathroom, and scampered back downstairs.

As she re-entered the living room, she heard Maddy explaining to the other two her bike situation, and expressing her opinions on what she should do about it. Aunt Caroline looked excited at the drama of it all, especially at the idea of a "stake-out" on the boardwalk in front of the bike rack. Zara, on the other hand, was no longer sitting primly upright, but was instead slumped down in her chair with an agonized expression on her face.

Aunt Caroline clapped her hands excitedly as Pam resumed her seat. "I think it's so exciting! You two are so brave! To think! Chasing down a bicycle thief!"

"Well," Pam said dryly, "I haven't exactly decided that that's what we're going to do!" She glared in Maddy's direction, but the other girl didn't seem to notice.

"I wonder," Aunt Caroline began, and trailed off looking thoughtful. The girls were respectfully silent as they thought that she was about to propose some plan of action for getting Pam's bike back. "I wonder," she said again, this time a little more hopefully. Suddenly, Aunt Caroline sat bolt upright, her frail body taut with excitement. "You know girls, maybe you can solve another problem–a sort of. . .well. . . mystery. Wouldn't that be nice?" Her eyes glistened. "The three of you could solve a puzzle that has been haunting me my whole life!" she cried dramatically, clapping again as if they'd already agreed.

Pam and Maddy looked up, interested. Zara had looked up too, at the phrase 'the three of you,' and frowned.

"What? What mystery?" Maddy asked excitedly.

"Well," Aunt Caroline began conspiratorially, "there was something in this house that was supposed to be special, or valuable, or. . .something." She paused, seeming hesitant and suddenly unsure.

"You mean a *treasure?*" Maddy squealed excitedly, practically exploding off of her chair.

"Yes, yes," Aunt Caroline said more confidently. "Yes, that's exactly what it was. A treasure."

Maddy was beside herself with the romance of it. Possibilities gleamed in her eyes. "What kind of treasure? From where? How do you know it's here?"

"Well," Aunt Caroline began, excited to have their full attention, "when I was a very little girl, I vaguely remember my parents hiding something here. It was something they brought back from a trip, and they hid it, they hid it *right here*."

"Wow!" both Pam and Maddy exclaimed. "But what was it? Why don't you know where it is? And why would they have hidden something valuable and not told anyone about it?" Pam asked.

Aunt Caroline's excitement dimmed for just a minute. "Because they died in a car crash not long after. On one of their trips. We were raised by nannies and grandparents before we were sent to boarding school. I suppose that if they hadn't died, they would have told someone about it." She sighed. "But the mystery of the treasure died with them."

Maddy's eyes positively glowed. Pam looked intrigued. The idea of solving this mystery appealed to her much more than Maddy's crazy scheme of catching the bicycle thief. The two girls looked around the room, considering each object in turn, pondering all the possible places where something might be hidden.

Maddy broke up the silence. "But how can we begin looking for something that could be, oh, I don't know, this little," she made a gesture with her fingers, "in a place as big as this!" As she spoke, she waved her arm around the room.

It was true. It would be like looking for a needle in a haystack.

"Well," began Aunt Caroline smugly, "I do have one clue."

The girls leaned forward. Even Zara could no longer pretend that she was alone in the room.

"I remember, the night I heard my parents shuffling around in their bedroom upstairs, talking secretively about something special, something they had to hide, that I heard the phrase 'under the cupola' several times." She shrugged and winked. "So we just have to figure out what they put under the cupola, and also which cupola they were talking about."

"Aunt Caroline," Zara began with a considerable edge in her voice, "there's only *one* cupola."

At the sound of Zara's voice, Pam looked up, startled. Was she the only one who thought it was strange that this was the first time this idiot had spoken? But as she looked around the table, she saw no sign that anyone saw anything unusual.

Aunt Caroline was speaking, though, rather triumphantly. "That's what *you* think. There was another one on the other half of the house that we lost track of after *this* house was moved."

"Whaaaat!" All three girls shouted at once. "This is only *half* a house?" Maddy asked, incredulous.

"Yep. Half a house. Have another piece of cake, and I'll tell you the story."

Chapter Nine

Six hands sunk eagerly into more cake and icing. Aunt Caroline paused dramatically until the three girls had filled their plates and looked ready to listen.

"Well," she said, somewhat breathless at having such a captive audience, "many, many years ago, this house was originally standing in South Cape May. . ."

"No way!" Pam interrupted, excited by this news. "South Cape May is now under water," she informed the others matter-of-factly.

"That's right!" Aunt Caroline added, nodding and winking.

"What? What do you mean 'under water'?" asked Maddy, puzzled.

Pam took over. "A long, long time ago, there was a place in Cape May called South Cape May. It was the last section of this town to be built. It's between the end of the boardwalk and the lighthouse," she said to her listeners, as if they understood exactly where that was. "Lots of houses used to be there."

"Yeah, and. . ." Maddy said, encouraging Pam to get on with it. "What happened?"

"Storms!" Aunt Caroline pronounced loudly.

"Yeah, storms," Pam repeated flatly, as if that explained everything.

"You mean, storms just came and washed all the houses away?" Maddy asked in a tone of disbelief, trying to flesh out the story. "That's weird. Why wouldn't the storms have washed away any of the other houses in town? Why just in that one spot?"

Pam looked at her half annoyed, and shrugged. "I don't know. They just didn't. I'll ask my Dad."

"But how did *this* house survive, and how did it get *here*?" asked Maddy, beginning to lose her patience.

"My grandparents moved it!" the little old lady said proudly.

"This huge house?" Maddy shouted. "Come on!" Even Zara looked skeptically at her aunt, who just sat there, blinking.

"No really, lots of houses have been moved in Cape May. Big ones, too," Pam said as she took a bite of cake. "We have picture books in our library that show houses on big flatbed trucks being moved down Beach Drive. They look funny, so huge and tall, sitting on a truck."

Maddy looked doubtful. "Really," Pam continued. "Some time when you're over, you can see the pictures."

"Whatever," Maddy said. "But Aunt Caroline, you said that this was half a house. What do you mean?"

The little old lady scrunched up her shoulders. "That's because it's true. When this house was moved, it was too big to move in one piece. So they divided it into two pieces, and moved each piece at a time. *This* house," she said looking around, and blinking, "is one of the pieces."

They all looked around, trying to imagine the house even bigger.

"Wow," Maddy and Pam said simultaneously.

"So what about the other half? Where is it?" Maddy asked.

Aunt Caroline blinked many times, and then shrugged. "Don't know! Lost!"

"Whaaaat?" Maddy shouted. "How could that even happen? I mean, did the truck carrying that half take a wrong turn somewhere, and the house got put in the wrong place? Or did it just fall off, and they decided to leave it there? What?"

Pam looked curious too. "Yeah, I mean how could that happen? You don't just lose a house. It doesn't make any sense."

"Well," Aunt Caroline began slowly, looking perplexed, "I have no idea. Come to think of it, they never told me that. You see, it was my grandparents' house, my grandparents on my mother's side. It was their summer house, and we only went for visits. When my parents died, we didn't come as often. Then one summer we came down here for vacation only to find that the house was in a completely different place, right where we are now, and smaller. The whole back end was gone. And they told me and my brother and sister what I just told you. And that's it! I guess we just never asked about the other half."

"Your grandparents must have moved it just in time before the storms wiped out South Cape May!" Pam exclaimed admiringly.

"But how could they have known the storms were coming?" Maddy wailed. "This story is confusing!"

"No, it *does* make sense," Pam said. "South Cape May got wiped out gradually. It wasn't just one storm, but many that did the trick. Your grandparents," Pam said, directing her remark to the older lady, "probably saw other houses get wrecked, and decided to move theirs inland. It makes perfect sense."

"Hm," Maddy said. "Well, okay." She shrugged. "But for somebody who doesn't read books, you sure do know a lot about this town."

Pam shrugged. "I live here."

There was a pause as they all digested the story. Suddenly, from out of nowhere, Zara shouted, "But what about the *CUPOLA*!!"

Pam looked at her, startled. Wow! Her second sentence! She looked at the others again, to see if they saw anything amiss. But no, as before, it was business as usual. Pam shook her head involuntarily. This girl was bizarre. And so were the rest of them for putting up with it.

Maddy took up the question. "That's right! And the treasure! Where is it?"

"Hm," Aunt Caroline said helplessly. "I'm not sure. All I know is, it's under the cupola."

"Well," Pam began, wanting to get down to business, "it's either under the cupola on the roof of *this* house, or under the cupola of the one that's *lost*. And if the treasure is in the house that was lost, we have a problem. I mean, that house could be *anywhere*! It could even have been demolished!"

"Oh, no!" Maddy wailed. "I want a treasure hunt! And the treasure!" Then, after a brief pause, "By the way, what's a cupola?"

Aunt Caroline opened her mouth to answer, but nothing came out. She closed it again, and blinked.

"It's a little lookout thing on the roof of some Victorian houses," Pam explained. "You can sometimes get into one if there are stairs leading up into it, and if it's really big, you can sit in it, and have a look around. One of my school friends has one on her house. It's really great for playing spies."

Maddy laughed, and Aunt Caroline nodded vigorously in agreement.

"Yes," the old lady said, "and both of ours had stairs,

stairs that folded down."

"You mean, like a trapdoor?" Pam asked.

The old lady nodded again. "Yes, yes. We should go upstairs to the one in the attic. It has a bench around it. I'm sure we could all fit." And to Pam she added, winking, "We also used it for playing spies."

"But didn't you hear '*under* the cupola'?" Maddy asked. "If a cupola is on the roof, what does that mean? Where could the treasure be hidden? After all, the whole *house* is under the cupola!"

Pam looked at Maddy with dawning admiration. "You're right. I never thought of that."

They all sat there lost in thought. Truthfully, it made no sense.

"Maybe," Aunt Caroline began hopefully, "we could start by exploring the attic. Maybe we'll find a clue there."

Maddy's eyes sparkled. She looked at Pam and Zara. "Let's do it! Right now! What do you say? What do we have to lose?"

"Right now?" Pam exclaimed. "Are you kidding? I have to go to work tonight!" She looked around for a clock. "In fact, I probably have to get going now. What time is it?"

Aunt Caroline peered intently at her watch, not really seeing anything but the sparkle of diamonds.

Maddy glanced up from hers. "Five-forty. Gosh,

don't you have to be at work at six?"

Pam exploded out of her chair. "I've got to run! Thanks for everything!" she threw over her shoulder, as she flew out of the room, through the hallway, and out the front door. She would barely have time for a bite of dinner.

Her mother greeted her as Pam stormed into the kitchen. "So how *was* it," she said meaningfully, with a curious grin.

"Not now, mom," Pam said with exaggerated patience. "I've got to get ready and go to work. Tomorrow, I promise. I'll tell you all about it at breakfast."

Her mom sighed, and patted Pam on the shoulder. "Run upstairs and get changed. "I'll make you a sandwich to take with you."

"Thanks, mom," Pam shouted over her shoulder as she raced upstairs.

Chapter 10

The smell of bacon greeted her on the stairs as Pam descended to breakfast, her stomach growling furiously. Last night's sandwich had been a pitiful bulwark against hunger. And after so much cake and icing all afternoon, Pam hadn't felt the urge to sample from her tray once. That meant that this morning all she could think about was filling up the empty cavern inside, and her stomach was roaring in agreement.

As she entered the kitchen she saw that both of her parents had frying pans in their hands and were busy at the stove.

"What are you making?" Pam asked, sliding into her seat at the round table, grabbing a knife and fork with each hand.

"Eggs."

"Bacon and sausage."

"What, no pancakes?" Pam cried.

Her father turned around, and peered at her over the top of his glasses.

Pam put her head face-down onto her plate, and banged her knife and fork on the table. "I'm star-ving,

I'm star-ving," she chanted in rhythm with her banging.

"Keep it up, and I'll add some dandelions to these eggs."

"Ugh!" This threat of her father's had been a running joke ever since she had complained about having to weed so many dandelions out of the yard.

"At least you don't have to eat them," her father had replied to her complaints. And he had gone on to tell her about how, a long time ago, people had eaten them because they were cheap and nutritious. They would even put them in sandwiches. Imagine–a dandelion sandwich!

"Ugh!" Pam said again with a shudder. Still talking into her plate, she said, "Mom, if after the bacon, sausages, and eggs I'm still hungry, can I please have some pancakes? Puh-leeze?" she begged.

"Pam!" her mother said sharply, "Get your head out of that plate. I sure do hope you had better manners next door."

"Ugh!" She was too hungry to even roll her eyes.

"Which reminds me," her mother said, coming over to the table with the frying pan, "how *was* it?"

"Great," Pam said robotically into her plate. "I'll tell you about it as soon as I know I'm not going to die of starvation."

"Well, do you want me to put these on the back of your head?"

Pam's head shot up like lightening, and she eagerly watched as her mother put bacon and sausages on three plates. Her father followed them up with scrambled eggs, and soon they were all seated, eating.

At least, Mr. And Mrs. Fischer were eating. What Pam was doing more resembled shoveling, prompting her mother to put her hand on her arm.

"Slow down."

With a giggle, Pam started cutting and chewing in slow motion. Then she remembered something. "Okay, but what about the pancakes?"

"Will you please finish that before you start asking about a second course?" her father said sternly.

"O-kay," Pam said with a resigned sigh, "but I like to know that I have options."

Her mother sighed. Her father pointed with his fork toward the window. "Options? You want options? There's a whole yard full of options. Take your pick."

Throwing her head back against the chair, Pam groaned in frustration.

"Parents!" she cried.

"Kids!" her parents responded in unison.

"I'll tell you what," Mrs. Fischer said in her most deal-cutting voice. "I'll promise to make you some scrumptious, fluffy, golden pancakes, topped with slabs of heart-attack inducing butter, if you promise to tell me about next door, and make it good. *Good*, do you hear? I want details!"

Pam giggled, and nodded vigorously, her mouth full.

Soon, she launched into a detailed description of what she saw in the house next door, including every detail she could possibly think of that would be of interest to her mother.

Periodically, Mrs. Fischer, listening intently with her brows furrowed, would break in with some comment such as, "Wow, gorgeous," or "Ooh, French provincial–hm, that's different," or "Hm. A china chandelier? Must be Capidomonte. Expensive, but I never would have thought they'd have anything so tacky," and so on. Eventually, when Pam had reached the end of her recital, and her mother had sufficiently "oohed" and "aahed" over their neighbor's house, she told her about their plans for rummaging through the attic. Mrs. Fischer's eyes were practically bulging out of their sockets.

"Really?" she cried in disbelief. "You've actually been invited to *do* that?"

"Yeah. We're looking for a treasure."

"Any particular *sort* of treasure?" her mom asked, trying to sound casual.

"Naw. It's just some idea that the old lady"--her mother frowned–"the old *woman* who owns the place has."

"Oh." Her mother looked as if she were about to ask another question, but Mr. Fischer broke in.

"Calm down, Linda, calm down. Don't even *think* about inviting yourself along."

"I wasn't going to," Mrs. Fischer said a bit huffily. "I was only excited about the possibilities. That attic is probably jam-packed with goodies. I mean, think of the things those people found in the attic of *Southern Mansion*." Mrs. Fischer was referring to one of Cape May's largest mansions that had just been renovated. Formerly, it had been a junked up, run down, old haunted house with hippies squatting in it, but the people who bought it sure did find a heap of valuable old things in it once they cleared out the mess.

Mrs. Fischer was gazing dreamily out the window, clearly imagining herself knee-deep in attic treasures, when there was a knock at the door.

"Come in!" Pam and her parents shouted at once.

Maddy came bouncing in, all smiles. Even though she hadn't been there for a week, she was greeted as a familiar early morning fixture at their table, so naturally Mrs. Fischer pressed breakfast on her.

"Well. . ." Maddy pretended to hesitate as her eyes scanned the table hungrily.

"No, really," Mrs. Fischer said. "I'm just about ready to throw some pancakes on. Right, Pam?"

Pam nodded vigorously in agreement.

"Have some orange juice in the meantime," Mr. Fischer offered, as his wife bustled about at the stove.

"Okay," Maddy consented happily, and pulled up a chair.

So while Mrs. Fischer cooked, Maddy filled Pam's parents in on their plans to root around in the attic, and why. She explained the whole story, and added that Aunt Caroline had always been haunted by this idea that her parents had hidden a treasure in the house. But, unfortunately, no one in her family had ever believed her. Apparently, according to Zara, Aunt Caroline's older sister was really mean, and wouldn't even let her younger sister mention the idea in her presence. But now that she was really getting on in years, she wanted to know for sure. It was now or never.

"I think Aunt Caroline is glad that it's just her and Zara in the house right now," Maddy confided. "Zara's grandmother is as mean as an army sergeant, and she would never let us explore the attic, let alone for this reason."

Mr. Fischer broke in. "You know, after you explore the attic, why not look around in our little library here. We have plenty of books about Cape May that we bought for guests. I know that some of them have photos of South Cape May, and even pictures of homes devastated by hurricane. One of them might mention some of the houses that were moved, and where they got to."

"Great!" Maddy exclaimed, thrilled that they were

all taking it seriously. "Thanks so much! Maybe after we do the attic today, we can come over tomorrow and look through the books!"

Pam suddenly looked up. "Today?" she asked.

"Yes, why not?"

Pam couldn't think of one good reason why not except that she hated being indoors on a bright sunny day. But then again, there was no other way to do an attic hunt.

"Oh, and another thing. Could Zara and I visit you at the candy store some night? Zara was asking about it, and she was, well, curious about your job and all."

Pam's fork stopped in mid-air. *Oh brother! That snotty little turd seeing me in that apron, holding out a tray of fudge? Yikes! What could be worse? Where will this end?*

"Oh, I guess so," she said ungraciously.

"Great!" Maddy said enthusiastically.

Just then, Mrs. Fischer plopped steaming pancakes on both of their plates.

"Satisfied?" she asked.

Two heads bobbed up and down.

Chapter Eleven

Pam walked up the path to the house next door for the second day in a row. It was just after midday, and both she and Maddy had just had one of the biggest lunches ever, provided by Mrs. Fischer, who was just as excited at the idea of her attic treasure hunt as Pam was.

Aunt Caroline and Zara were sitting on the porch swing, chatting. Pam wondered what they could be talking about. At least she doesn't give that nice old lady the silent treatment, Pam reflected. But before she could pursue her thoughts concerning this strange girl any further, Maddy had bounded up the stairs and pounced on the quiet pair.

"Zara! Aunt Caroline!" Maddy cried, flinging herself on the two of them, and setting the swing violently in motion.

It wasn't the first time that Pam wondered how the silent and aloof Zara had ended up with a bouncing puppy of a friend like Maddy. Maddy seemed to embody everything that a girl like Zara would find annoying. She just didn't get it. But, oh well, thought

Pam, as she watched Zara calmly extricate herself from Maddy's embrace, you just never know.

Today Pam had dressed in clothes she might weed in. The little old lady, on the other hand, was dressed completely in pink, and what with that and the mound of snow white hair on her head, she looked exactly like a pink and white fairy.

"Um," Pam said to her, unsure how to proceed without offending, "attics are sort of, well, dirty." She figured that would be enough of a hint.

Aunt Caroline beamed in response. "Oh I know, I know. It's going to be dusty up there. It's *never* cleaned, and it's *packed*. Absolutely *packed*. My brother and sister and I have been using that attic for years as storage. Isn't it thrilling?" She nodded vigorously, and shrugged her shoulders rapidly with excitement.

Pam wasn't exactly sure which part was thrilling, but she nodded her head in agreement anyway. The little old lady motioned them all toward the front door. "Come on, come on," she said excitedly. "Let's get our adventure started!"

The four of them traipsed up the grand staircase to the second floor, and then up a narrower one to the third floor, the entirety of which, apparently, was the attic. The door at the top of the stairs was stuck, and there seemed to be no other choice but for Pam and Maddy to use their shoulders as battering rams. After a few tries, the door suddenly gave way, and the two girls stumbled into a dark, hot, stuffy, airless space.

"Ugh! Aunt Caroline!" Zara whined. "We can't go in there!"

The intensity of the heat sucked their breath away. It was suffocating. They all hesitated at the door, but Pam, an experienced attic explorer, knew exactly what to do.

"Come on! We just have to open some of the windows and get some air in here."

Pam took a flashlight out of her pocket, and switched it on, silently thanking her mom for reminding her to bring it. She passed the light over the crowded room, and noticed that there were many dormer windows, tall and narrow, with criss-crossing panes, that could probably be opened. The problem was getting to them, for this attic was packed to the rafters with *stuff*.

Pam started to make her way carefully toward a window at the side of the house. She gingerly moved around boxes and piles of whatnot, finally squeezing behind a chest that had been placed in front of the window. She started working on the window frame, jiggling it in and out, but gently, because it was clearly old. She tapped around the frame, as she had seen her father do when he had tried to raise a stuck window, and at last, she loosened it enough for it to slide up.

A cool rush of air met her eager face, and she breathed deeply. It was a hot day outside, but the window was level with the tops of the trees, and there was a gentle breeze rustling through them. In comparison with the attic, the warm air from outside was glorious. She was reluctant to move away from the window.

"I feel it! I feel some air!" Maddy cried. "Let me do one!"

Maddy plunged headlong into another group of boxes, knocking something over as she hastened toward a faint glimmer of light in another part of the room. Zara and Aunt Caroline just stood by the door.

"I can't get it, it's stuck," Maddy wailed. "Ew. It's so stuffy I can't breathe."

"Just rattle it back and forth, and then tap around the edges with your fist. Just don't miss and hit a window pane. They might pop out or something."

Soon, accompanied by a lot of grunting, Pam and Maddy had opened most of the windows except one, which wouldn't give way for either of them. But it didn't matter. The air in the room had begun to cool and even circulate a bit. At least they could all breathe.

As Pam passed the flashlight around the room, all four of them realized for the first time the enormity of the task before them. Even Aunt Caroline was silent.

"What is it we're supposed to be looking for again?" Maddy asked with a giggle.

Pam laughed. "Um, I think we're looking for. . .a clue to what's, er, 'under the cupola'!"

"Oh, right," Maddy said nodding. Then, after a pause, "So where's the cupola?"

Aunt Caroline pointed upward, to a spot on the ceiling in the middle of the room. Pam turned her flashlight on it, and they all peered intently at a large square outlined in the ceiling.

"Oh, I know, I remember!" Aunt Caroline suddenly said, excited once again. She pushed the attic door closed a bit, and fumbled around behind it. She reemerged with a metal rod about three feet in length. "Here, use this," she said, as she handed it eagerly to Pam.

Pam looked at the rod, looked at Aunt Caroline, and then looked up at the ceiling. Just visible was a small metal loop at one end of the square in the ceiling. Pam then looked at the rod, and noticed that it had a hook at one of its ends. She held the rod up to the ceiling, and after quite a few misses, managed to finally hook it into the loop.

"Whew! My arms are tired!" She let the rod dangle for a minute as she shook out her arms.

"Okay, here goes!" She yanked on the rod. The trap door opened slowly at first, creaking in reluctance. Then, it fell open in a rush, letting in a sudden burst of sunshine so bright it made their eyes water.

Wooden steps were folded up neatly inside, and since there happened to be nothing on the floor at that spot, Maddy and Pam pulled them down together.

Aunt Caroline was beside herself with excitement.

"Wow," Maddy exclaimed looking up. "It's a skylight that you can get into."

"Come on, let's go up," Pam said eagerly as she started to climb. They all followed her lead, and soon, all four of them were up inside the cupola, seated on the bench that surrounded it, looking out the windows on all sides at the spectacular view.

It was fabulously bright up there, for the roof was level with the tops of even the highest trees. And from their extra height, they could easily see over the roofs of the houses on either side. Pam looked at her own rooftop curiously. In silence, they turned this way and that, seeing nothing but blue sky above and green foliage below.

Suddenly, Pam exclaimed, "Look! Look at the ocean!" And all eyes turned in the direction of the beach.

A sailboat with billowing white sails on three masts was gliding slowly past on the horizon.

"It's beautiful!" Pam gushed in admiration. "I *love* sailboats. Isn't it great?"

Aunt Caroline beamed with joy at being in her lookout once again. "I haven't been up here in years!"

she exclaimed, her blue eyes sparkling in the bright light. "No one has ever wanted to come up here with me." She looked at the girls in gratitude, her eyes blinking thanks.

"Ick!" Pam said, wiping the window with the back of her hand for a clearer view. "These windows are filthy. No one's cleaned up here in years, either," she said, as she held up the back of her hand for them all to see. As she did so, she glanced up at the ceiling of the cupola itself.

"Hey, look. It's been painted."

Everybody looked up, and sure enough, the cupola ceiling was painted with gold stars which shimmered against a midnight blue background.

"Neat," Pam said. "Who did that?"

"Ah," Aunt Caroline said, sighing. "The night sky. I remember that." She clasped her hands together in front of her. "Beautiful."

"Yeah, it's nice," Pam agreed. "But who did it? And why?"

"Oh. . .my mother, most likely." She peered at the faded ceiling intently. "I can't believe that has survived all this time. It must be more than sixty years old, at least."

"Was she glamorous?" Maddy asked, completely out of the blue. "I love glamour."

"Yes, oh yes, she was," the old lady reminisced. "She

was very, very beautiful, a notorious beauty from what my grandmother told me. And then she was always traveling, to Europe, to exotic places. And coming back with things, you know. Valuable things." She paused, deep in her memories. The girls remained quiet.

Suddenly, her back straightened, and her gaze came sharply into focus. "*That's* why I know there's something here, something special. There was always something that she brought home, but once there was something different from all of the other things. That's why they had to hide it. And that's what I heard them talking about, one night when I was supposed to be in bed. They were hiding it, hiding it 'under the cupola,' 'under the cupola,'" she chanted. "It meant something," she cried, "I know it did. But no one believes me!"

"*We* believe you," Pam said firmly. "We just don't know where to look. I mean, 'under the cupola' is just a spot on the floor." All four heads leaned over, and looked down through the hole in the floor, to where the stairs of the trap door rested on the floor. It just didn't make any sense.

"And we don't even know if this is the *right* cupola," Maddy added. They all sighed.

After they had sat in a depressed silence for a few minutes, Pam said, "Look. We're not getting anything done just sitting here. We've got to rummage around for a clue. Who knows? Maybe we'll find something else that's valuable. I mean, this place looks like an *Antiques Roadshow* bonanza!"

She spoke with energy, but the others lagged behind in their enthusiasm. Nobody moved.

"Come *on*," she insisted, starting down the stairs. "Let's *go*."

They followed her lead, and once down on the attic floor, they all agreed that the trap door should remain open to let in light. Of course, that meant that they could all see quite clearly how daunting the task was before them. Maddy let out a sigh, and the ever-silent Zara looked like she was wondering how she had ever let herself get involved in this mess in the first place.

"Okay," Pam began, rubbing her hands together. "There are four of us. Let's divide the attic into four parts. We'll each go through one section and see what we come up with."

They all agreed with the plan, or at least no one seemed to disagree with it, but Maddy asked, "How do we know when we've found something valuable?"

"Oh, I don't know. You just have to guess." Then Pam added wistfully, "Boy, do I wish my mom were here. She'd know in a second."

Pam designated the sections, and told them to get started. Zara looked at her with her mouth open, as if she were about to object, but Pam just turned abruptly away.

"Aye, aye, sir," Maddy playfully responded, saluting.

"Hey, you asked me here," Pam retorted.

All the rest of the afternoon they worked, although Maddy, Zara, and Aunt Caroline occasionally needed reminding as to why they were there in the first place. They would sort diligently for a little while, and then get distracted by something–old clothes, old toys, and then finally, a box of old costume jewelry that even roused Zara's interest.

"May I take these to my room and look through them later?" she asked her aunt, referring to the jewelry box and a very tattered old book.

"Of course, dear, of course," Aunt Caroline answered absent-mindedly, holding up an old fancy dress to herself, fitting it around her tiny frame.

And so that was how it went the rest of the day. Pam methodically examined every inch of her area; the others got thoroughly caught up in just looking at the stuff. By late afternoon, all that they could say they found that would be of any help to their treasure hunt was an old photo album that had pictures of Aunt Caroline and her siblings when they were children. Pam thought that this was a good find, because some of the pictures would reveal some clue to what the house had looked like a long time ago, when it was all in one piece. So Maddy, gleeful that it was she who had discovered it, put it by the attic door.

By four o'clock, they had seen plenty of old clothes, furniture, jewelry, children's games, sports equipment, and books—everything that would be of interest to an attic-junk enthusiast—but nothing that even remotely resembled a treasure.

Eventually, they had to admit defeat. Pam had to go to work, and light in the attic was fading. They closed the windows, put up the cupola stairs, gathered up the things they wanted to examine later, and trudged down to the cooler levels below.

Aunt Caroline looked sad as she led Pam to the front door. Disappointment was etched on her wrinkled, old face.

"Thank you, my dear," she said, blinking more slowly than usual. "I hope *you* aren't terribly disappointed."

"Don't worry," Pam reassured the little old woman. "We'll find something yet. Just think," she added, trying to be optimistic, "it's probably right under our noses, only we just can't see it." She shook the old woman's hand, smiled quickly, and then turned and sped down the porch steps and on over to her own house for a clean-up before dinner. A *proper* dinner, this time.

Chapter Twelve

L ater on that day, Pam was having one of her worst nights ever at the *Chocolate Pot*. The old grouch was in an especially bad mood (if that was possible) and Pam was getting yelled at for everything. She had even just then been yelled at for the fact that there were no customers in the store.

To top it off, as soon as she had gotten into position by the shop door, Pam was certain that she had seen her bike go by with the same fair-haired rider perched on its seat, bicycling casually, looking as though she hadn't a care in the world. Pam followed the bike with her eyes until it was out of sight, frustrated beyond belief to be anchored to where she stood. In fact, she was so frustrated with everything right now, she felt downright miserable. All that time spent on that stupid attic, she thought, and I haven't even worked on my own problem. Meanwhile, I stand here like an idiot, being yelled at by a mean old witch, trying to earn money for a bike just because some selfish creep couldn't keep her hands off mine. And to top it off, she thought angrily, I have to keep *seeing* her. She felt like plopping down on one of the boardwalk benches and letting loose sobs or screams, whichever came out first.

Even the tourists were a pain tonight. One woman complained that Pam didn't have enough variety on her tray. Another tourist stood there munching for so long, that he ate most of what was there. As he stood there "sampling," Pam stared at him, open-mouthed in disbelief. What could she say? He was a grown up. But she was sure that she was going to hear about this one.

And sure enough, as soon as the man finally dragged himself away, the shop door was roughly pushed open.

"Whatdya doin'?"Ya can't let 'em eat up all the samples! Ya won't have any left for the rest of the night! *No refills!*" the old woman poked her finger threateningly in Pam's direction, "till seven fifteen. *Seven fifteen,*" she repeated. The door slammed shut.

Pam looked at the few scattered cubes of fudge on her tray and wondered how they would last for another three-quarters of an hour. If they don't, what will I do? she wondered. Just stand here with an empty tray?

Stinging tears of frustration began to well up in her eyes. The back of her throat started to smart. All of the energy and optimism she had spent on bolstering other people's spirits all day had left her, and there was none for herself. Who was going to lift *her* spirits? Who was around to sympathize with *her* woes?

She lifted the arm of her shirt sleeve and caught

a couple of tears before they rolled down her cheeks. She had to watch it, or pretty soon the tourists would notice—and wouldn't *that* be pathetic!

Just then, she saw two familiar figures a short way down the boardwalk. She stared in disbelief, with tears starting to well up even more. Pam wasn't sure whether it was because she felt a comforting relief at seeing a friend (Maddy), or irritation at seeing a definite non-friend (Zara). She wiped her eyes again, and stood there with glistening lashes as the two girls came toward her.

Maybe they won't notice, Pam thought, as she squeezed her eyes shut and opened them wide a couple of times in a row. And if they do, I'll simply say that the sun's in my eyes.

"Oh Pam!" Maddy exclaimed as she rushed up to her. "You're crying! What's the matter?" she said so sympathetically, that Pam became choked up all over again, and this time she really had to struggle to fight back the tears. She tried to speak, but couldn't get a sound out of her mouth.

Maddy patted her kindly on her shoulder. "Oh Pam, is it. . .is it that mean old lady?" she asked, her head bobbing in sympathy.

"No. . .it's. . .it's. . . the sun," Pam insisted, "the sun. . .it's . . .in my eyes," she sputtered, unable to go on, putting her arm up to shield her eyes from the sun, and blinking rapidly. Zara just stood there, her enormous brown eyes just staring. Pam felt too miserable to care.

"Do you want me to hold the tray for you tonight?" Maddy asked. "I can do it. Then you could just go home and relax. We had such a long day today." Maddy nodded emphatically at every word, her hands resting at her waist. "Really. Let me take over for you."

Pam giggled in spite of herself, warmed by Maddy's kind offer. "Uh, I don't know. It's a special skill, holding this tray. You've got to do it just right. I'm really not sure you have what it takes."

The two girls laughed, which for Pam, released some of her pent-up tension. Meanwhile, Zara continued standing off to the side, as still and silent as a statue.

Pam realized for the first time as she looked at Maddy, standing there expectantly, still waiting for Pam to hand her the tray, that she wasn't just some silly, annoying girl who was interfering with her summer plans. She was a good friend who meant well, even if she was a bit spacey sometimes.

Pam shook her head seriously. "No. I know that I wouldn't be allowed to do that. But thanks," she said firmly, really meaning it. "But why are you guys here?" she asked. She knew that if Maddy and Zara stood there much longer, the old woman would be out the door barking at her, but she just had to know.

"Well, we were wondering if we could come over tomorrow and look in your library like your Dad suggested. You see," Maddy went on, "we looked through the photo album and there are some pictures of the house, but in a different place. So Zara's aunt must be right. It's probably South Cape May. Maybe if we look through those history books, we'll find some information that'll help us. You never know," Maddy finished, shrugging.

Pam perked up. The idea didn't seem so bad. Even the idea of Zara being there didn't seem so terrible. She stole a glance at that impassive face. Jeesh, Pam thought, I must be depressed.

"Sounds good," she said aloud.

"Great!" Maddy cried. "Aunt Caroline wants to come too. Is that okay?"

"Fine," Pam said, laughing at the idea of their seventy year old tag-a-long friend. "Of course it's okay."

"I'm glad. She's all upset right now." Maddy hesitated for a second, but then continued. "She got a call from her sister, you know, Zara's grandmother, who's thinking of coming down to the shore. That got Aunt Caroline all upset."

Pam was about to ask why, wondering what Aunt Caroline's sister's visit had to do with looking for clues, or why it would make her upset, when all of a sudden, the shop door exploded open.

The door opened so quickly, with such a sudden burst of air, and the old woman barked so fiercely, that the three girls shrieked, and the tray itself went flying up into the air, sending the few remaining cubes of fudge in every direction. Finally, after what seemed like an eon, the tray came crashing down, face down on the boardwalk at Pam's feet.

Pam and the two girls just stared at it. Suddenly, it seemed like flames from a raging fire were coming out of the old woman's mouth as she launched into a blistering tirade against Pam, her friends, dumb kids, tourists, lazy employees, and everything else under the summer sun that met with her severe disapproval.

Tourists started to stare, and cluck sympathetically at the trio of unfortunate girls who were clearly the object of the old woman's wrath.

The girls themselves just stood there, mouths open, staring in amazement at the venomous old woman. Finally finished with her harangue, the old woman snapped in Pam's direction, "Take off that apron. You're *fired*!"

That last word split through the summer evening like a streak of lightening. Not quite realizing what she was doing, and numb with shock, Pam started to unfasten her apron strings.

Maddy, coming to her senses first, started to

expostulate. "But we weren't. . .we didn't mean to. . .we were just. . ." But the old woman cut her off.

"Get going!" she snapped curtly to the three of them. She snatched the apron out of Pam's hands, and picked up the tray from the boardwalk. One last time, the door slammed behind her.

The three girls were in a daze. Pam couldn't even get her legs moving.

"Oh, Pam! I'm so sorry! It's all my fault!" Maddy cried, wringing her hands. "I had no idea it was *that* bad!"

"Neither did I!" Pam said.

The girls started to move down the boardwalk.

"Let's go home," Maddy said gently. "You can come over to Aunt Caroline's and have a cup of tea, and stay until you're ready to face your parents. Come on."

Pam thanked her, but said she'd prefer to go home and crawl straight into her bed.

"That makes sense," Maddy said nodding. "That's what I do after I've had a day like this."

Pam wondered uncharitably for just a second how many days Maddy had actually had like this, but then put the thought aside. She knew her friend was just trying to be sympathetic, and that was all that mattered.

The three girls made their way down the boardwalk towards home, Pam still in a complete daze. Occasionally, Zara would look sideways at her, and stare, but she still said nothing.

Chapter Thirteen

Books were spread out everywhere on the floor. Mr. Fischer was pulling them off the shelves faster than he could even read the titles out to the small group now assembled in the little library. He was so excited that these books that he had bought for tourists were finally going to be used, that anything even remotely relating to the history of Cape May was headed for a growing pile in the center of the room.

The Fischer's library was the smallest room in the house, tucked away just behind the living room. It was almost as small as a large walk-in closet, but it was packed with books and comfy furniture. Built-in bookshelves lined each wall, crammed with books so that restless tourists would have something to occupy themselves with in the unlucky event of summer showers. It was simply the perfect little hide-away in which to curl up and read, or, as in Pam's case, to day-dream.

Mr. Fischer finally decided the pile was high enough, and, with a big grin, wished them all luck on his way out. The girls started sorting through the pile, selecting titles that might relate to their search, while

Aunt Caroline sat patiently on the sofa. The books covered a range of subjects, including Victorian architecture, landscaping ("Good grief, more weeding," Pam said when she saw it), the history of New Jersey, the history of Cape May, and even New Jersey storms.

Pam balked. "We've got to read all this?" she yelled.

Maddy laughed. "No. Just bits and pieces, you know, like when you do research for a school research paper."

Pam just looked at her.

"You *have* written a research paper, right?" Maddy asked with a giggle.

"I *guess* so."

Some unflattering sound came from Zara's direction. Pam turned toward her sharply with a frown, but Maddy quickly went on. "Zara, remember those essays on ancient Egypt we did for Mrs. Goodman last year?" Not waiting for a response, as Zara seemed to be already absorbed in a book, Maddy turned back to Pam. "I did mine on Bastet, the cat goddess. Zara did hers on Nefertiti. Anyway, the point is, you use the index to look for what you want to read about, so that you don't have to read a whole book just for one little fact." Maddy opened the back of the book at the index, which was completely new to Pam, and showed her how to look something up by using the tiny page references.

After paying close attention to what Maddy was showing her, and nodding as if in complete understanding, Pam suddenly shouted "Torture!" and rolled over backwards moaning.

Maddy giggled at the look Zara gave Pam as she rolled around on the floor, pretending to be in the throes of agony.

"Come on, you can do it," Maddy said, nudging Pam. "Remember how you got us going with the attic yesterday? Well, come on!"

But Pam retorted, "Thanks, but I think I'd rather go exploring in a hot, dark, dusty attic than do all that index stuff."

But she sat upright anyway, and started sorting through the books, albeit reluctantly, looking for one that would produce the least agony.

Soon, everyone had a book to examine except Aunt Caroline. Zara, nestled into a corner of the plush sofa, seemed to be thoroughly carried away by hers, so Maddy helped Aunt Caroline choose one. Eventually they settled on a big picture book of famous Cape May houses.

They all began to read, or flip through their books, looking at pictures. Pam remained on the floor, having chosen a book on New Jersey storms as the most interesting. But she turned the pages as if they were blank, impatient for the whole project to be over. What she wished for more than anything, was for someone to suggest that they chuck all of this and go to the beach. But looking around at the other three, she knew they'd only laugh at her if she even suggested it. So she sighed and looked down, determined to concentrate. Periodically, they all looked up from their books to comment on some interesting tidbit that they'd read. Rarely did any of them refer to anything that was not about the subject at hand. Pam marveled at their discipline, but was also glad that they were all avoiding one subject in particular: the events of the night before at *The Chocolate Pot*.

When they had parted the evening before, Pam had made clear two things. The first was that they couldn't come over till after 10:30, when she'd be finished with her chores. The second thing was that they couldn't even mention that evening's events, just in case Pam hadn't yet gotten around to telling her parents that she'd been fired from her very first job. And sure enough, next morning she still hadn't gotten around to it.

As she stared at the pages before her, Pam's mind wandered, and, no matter how hard she tried to force it not to, it kept going back to the previous night. The knot that had been in her stomach since the moment the fudge tray went flying up into the air grew

even more painful as she remembered the embarrassing episode. And it wasn't just embarrassing. It
was hurtful and disappointing, too. Although she had
been paid Katy's allowance for two weeks already, she
could hardly expect any more, which meant that her
plans to get a new bike before the end of the summer were dashed, just like that. Not to mention the
fact that she was disappointing Katy *and* her parents.
Pam shuddered at the thought of Katy finding out how
things had turned out. She knew that having been fired
wasn't entirely her own fault, and that the old woman
was completely mean and nasty, but it didn't matter.
Everyone was going to be disappointed. And sooner
or later she was going to have to tell her parents what
had happened. At the thought, the knot tightened, and
she felt sick.

Whether it was because of misery at her situation,
or boredom with the book on storms, Pam simply
couldn't concentrate. She picked up the old photo
album that they had discovered in the attic and that
Zara had brought over at Maddy's insistence. The night
before, while seated on the porch swing with Maddy
and the still-silent Zara, Maddy had excitedly shoved
the album under Pam's nose. But she had certainly
not been in the mood to look at it then. Now, as she
looked closer at the old black and white photos, she
was amazed at how different the house had looked in

its earlier setting. South Cape May had been a barren, deserted landscape, without trees or shrubbery, or anything. It was just a flat track of land with houses lined up in a row on the ocean front with absolutely nothing else around. Pam couldn't even imagine why anyone would want to live in such an ugly place.

There was also a photograph of Aunt Caroline's mother, a formal, black and white portrait photo revealing a snobbish-looking young beauty in 1920's clothing looking insolently into the camera as if it were just the luckiest camera in the world to be pointed in her direction.

"Ha, it figures," muttered Pam to herself. Below the photo, written in old-fashioned, flowing script was her name:

Clara Von Schoenfeldt

She didn't look very nice. In fact, she had the same uppity air that Zara had, only with a more mischievous look in her eyes, as if she were up to no good, and was secretly amused by the fact.

There were other photos, too, photos of Clara's grand wedding to a Percival Huntington-Caldwell, a wedding which took place in a flower-bedecked church as big as a cathedral. As Pam pondered one photo of the wedding couple, with the bride's train trailing down the aisle behind them, she blurted out,

"So, they were rich?"

Everyone looked up rather confused, as the question came out of nowhere. When they all realized what she was referring to, Zara frowned in disapproval, and Maddy giggled as usual. Only Aunt Caroline seemed to think it was the most normal question in the world.

"Yes," she chirped brightly in response. "Yes, they were *quite* rich. My mother came from a wealthy German family which had settled in Philadelphia, where my father lived. His family was still in England, of course. They were a titled family. But he had come to America to start a new life for himself. So he went to University here, and afterwards, went into banking in the city. But even though he was only a younger son, he still had heaps of money." She sighed, her eyes gazing into the distance. "I wish we had known them. Such a stylish couple!"

Pam didn't know what to say to this. She thought it was the strangest reason to miss one's parents that she had ever heard, but as she looked at Maddy's face, as day-dreamy and misty as the old lady's, she decided to keep that opinion to herself.

She looked back down at the album, and flipped through pages and pages of pictures documenting what could only be described as an exceedingly glamorous life. The Huntington-Caldwell's had been photographed at one society event after another, and had visited friends in stately homes and castles of a size and extravagance that Pam had only seen in picture books. These faded black and white photos recorded not just another time, but a whole other world. Even Pam knew that the album was a piece of history, a personal glimpse into a time long past whose ways would never be seen again. What was weird was that everything in it seemed so far away, but right here, sitting on the sofa, was someone who was only one step away from that world. For this glamorous, globe-trotting young couple, socializing in the most elegant drawing-rooms and in the most exotic locales of the 1920's, was Aunt Caroline's *parents*. It was weird.

So the morning wore on, their work only interrupted occasionally by Mr. Fischer popping his head in the doorway, curious to know if they'd found anything yet. Apparently, Pam's parents were beginning to get excited about the "mystery" after all. Once, after one of his inquiries, Maddy couldn't resist asking Pam quietly, "What are you going to do tonight, when it's time to go?"

Pam just shrugged. She had absolutely no idea.

Aunt Caroline chirped loudly, "Go where?"

All three girls shushed her, and the little old lady fell silent, but with wide, wondering eyes.

After a while, Maddy asked Pam, "Shall I tell her?"

Pam shrugged again.

Maddy took this as a "yes," and so she proceeded to tell Aunt Caroline about Pam's having been fired, and why.

Aunt Caroline listened intently, but at one point broke in rather loudly with, "What's fired?"

All three heads turned toward her in amazement.

Zara said sharply, "Aunt Caroline, you don't know what "*fired*" means?"

Aunt Caroline just blinked. Just then, Mr. Fischer popped his head in again. The girls quickly looked down at their books. Aunt Caroline, however, was so obviously perplexed, that they were on pins and needles just waiting for her to ask Mr. Fischer what "fired" meant.

But she didn't, and after a few words of encouragement, Mr. Fischer popped back out. They all let out a sigh of relief, and started whispering all at once. Zara tried to explain.

"It's, like, when you have a job, but your boss tells you to go home."

"Like a vacation?" Aunt Caroline asked, blue eyes blinking.

Zara frowned, while Maddy giggled. "No, *not* like a vacation," Zara said impatiently.

"Well, actually, yes it is," Maddy contradicted her.

"It is like a vacation, except that it's a permanent one," she finished with a loud chuckle. "You don't ever return from it."

"Oh," Aunt Caroline responded nodding, "kicked out." Maddy giggled even harder at that. The old lady was silent for a minute, thinking. Then suddenly she said to Pam loudly, "You got kicked out?"

A chorus of "shushs" rained down on her white head, and Pam looked up at her with a crease between her brows.

"You could say that," she said flatly.

They all tried to resume reading. Suddenly, Zara broke the silence. "I think I've found something!" She was reading a book called *The Summer City By the Sea* by Emil R. Salvini that was an illustrated history of Cape May. Zara read aloud, starting in the middle of a sentence: "*excursion came down from Philadelphia of about 150 Germans, some of them interested in the Mt. Vernon Land Co's lots. . .*" She explained, "Apparently that was the name of South Cape May. And listen to this," she continued reading, "*The tract developed slowly into a small community of beach front cottages. Mt. Vernon was chartered as the borough of South Cape May in 1894. Never a major success, the community's distance from the City of Cape May's urban center proved troublesome. Erosion and savage storms raged a continuous battle for possession of the community until the weatherworn borough of South Cape May was finally dissolved in 1945. Many of the South Cape May homes were moved. . ."*

Zara looked up with an expression that almost seemed happy. "It may be true after all," she said surprised.

"Interesting," Pam said thoughtfully, getting up to look at the book over Zara's shoulder. "Before 1945, many of the houses *had* to be moved, whether people liked it or not."

Maddy bounced a couple of feet over on the sofa in order to get a closer look at Zara's book. The photographs in it revealed the same bleak, barren landscape that the photos in the album had shown, only in the book, some of the pictures were of houses that had been photographed after they'd been hit by storms. They looked wobbly and tilted, as if they were toy houses that had been stepped on, or models that had been sloppily built.

"Gosh," Maddy said. "It's a good thing it was moved, otherwise, this would be your beach house," she said, pointing to a particularly squashed one. She laughed out loud. Pam giggled at the thought of the uppity Zara living in such a ramshackle dwelling, but Zara herself was clearly not amused. She chose to ignore the other two.

"But my parents were gone before it was done," the old woman complained, "so their secret died with them. How can we find it? How can we find the house with the cupola that has the treasure?" she wailed.

"Well," Pam began, wanting to console the old woman, "we know from the book that Germans moved there, and your mother's family was German, so that fits. What we have to find out is what the other half of the house looked like, and where it might have gotten to."

"Hm," Maddy reflected. "Maybe we should get one of those bikes that four people can ride, and ride around in that section of town just to see if anything looks familiar."

"We *could*," Pam said doubtfully. "But people change their houses so much. I mean, look at what my parents did to this one. It looks completely different from how it was when they bought it."

The wind went temporarily out of their sails when they realized they still had nothing to go on.

"Oh, let's take the bike ride anyway," Pam said, not wanting to give in to the gloom, and happy with the idea of finally *doing* something–and getting outside. "You never know. Something's bound to turn up."

"May I come along too?" Aunt Caroline asked, blinking in expectation.

"Of course," Pam replied. "You *have* to come. They'll never rent a surrey to kids," she said matter-of-factly. Aunt Caroline beamed with excitement at her own importance.

"And Mike will have to come too," Pam added, referring to their house handyman. "We'll need someone who can pedal hard, because those bikes sure are heavy. Meanwhile, come on. My mom's prepared us all a big lunch."

Chapter Fourteen

About an hour later, three very stuffed eleven year old girls, one frail little old lady, and one lanky, suntanned youth carrying the remains of his last sandwich all scrambled out of the Fischer's car at a bicycle rental shop in the center of town.

At first, when they had discussed their plan over lunch, Pam and Maddy had insisted that they all walk to the bike shop, with even Aunt Caroline nodding her head vigorously in agreement, too excited to be included to think about anything mundane such as how far it was. After Zara pointed out with a frown that her Aunt didn't even know where or how far they were going, Mrs. Fischer intervened.

"How about if I drive all of you to the bike shop? After all," she said, looking meaningfully at Pam, her eyes flickering just perceptibly toward Aunt Caroline, "you don't want to tire yourselves out before your exploration, do you?"

Pam took the hint. Soon, everyone was persuaded that a car ride was the best idea, and so that is how, a little while later, they were all to be seen tumbling out of the Fischer's weather-beaten car and onto the sun-beaten parking lot where tourists were swarming around bikes of all shapes, colors, and sizes.

As they all walked around the gravel lot in between rows and rows of bikes all lined up with military precision, a couple of hands reached out for the handlebars of single bicycles, one more eagerly than all the rest.

Pam positively ached to have a bike to herself right then. She longed to grab one, and tear out of that lot as hard and fast as her legs could go. She wanted to feel that painful tightening in her thighs from pushing too hard, and to feel herself going faster and faster, and to smell the scents that always accompanied that effort— as if she had rushed headlong into the air and stirred up its warm summer scents of salt and sea, making them swirl around and around and finally engulf her.

But today it was not to be. Mike interrupted her daydream.

"Yo, dudes, what are ya' doin'?" Mike called to the group which had by now dispersed around the collection of bikes. "The bike we want is over here."

He gestured them over to their ride for the day, a four-wheeled contraption with a front and back seat, two steering wheels in the front, and enough pedals for everyone to get in on the action. Topping it off was a bright red canopy.

"It's almost as big as a car," Maddy said, her eyes

wide. They all just stood there looking at it dubiously.

Pam, too, was a little disappointed at first, but as it was blazing hot, she decided it might not be so bad to ride around under what was essentially a giant umbrella. She hopped into the driver's seat, and said, "Come on, try it out!" while the others still stood there, motionless.

"Naw, I'm in the driver's seat," Mike said. "You see how heavy this thing is?" He stood beside the surrey, grabbed hold of it with two hands, and pushed it forward. It barely moved a foot.

"See dude? It's heavy."

"But what do you mean? What difference does it make? There's a steering wheel for both of us," Pam argued.

"Dude, use your head. It's not just the steering. It's signaling and everything. I gotta be in the driver's seat," Mike maintained. "Anyway, here comes the guy."

"The guy" was the bike shop attendant, who walked over to their little group, looked at the girls, then at Aunt Caroline, raised both eyebrows, and said, "This bike is heavy."

"I know, I know. That's what I've been tryin' to tell 'em. But they won't listen," Mike said.

At that, all heads turned toward Pam, as if everyone understood that "they" actually meant "Pam." She stubbornly gripped the wheel.

"Twelve dollars for one hour, *you* drive," the attendant said to Mike, concluding the matter.

Mike pulled out his driver's license, and the girls reached into their pockets.

"How much is it?" Maddy asked. "Three, two-fifty, what?"

"Why don't we make it three each," Mike answered. "That way you'll ride for free," he said to Aunt Caroline winking. "Our treat."

That set off a series of winks, and blinks, and shrugs as she beamed back at him.

They all climbed in, Mike and Pam in the front, and Maddy and Zara in the back seat with Aunt Caroline, beside herself with excitement, perched between them.

As they all adjusted themselves, and got their feet on the peddles, Maddy giggled, and asked sheepishly for what seemed like the zillionth time, "What are we looking for again?"

Pam responded a little testily. "For anything that looks like the rest of Aunt Caroline's house, that's what! And we're also going to take a look at where South Cape May used to be, for, well. . .for. . ." she trailed off, unsure how to put it.

"Inspiration!" came the surprising reply from Aunt Caroline.

Pam whirled around. "Yes, that's it! Exactly!

Inspiration. I mean, maybe we'll just get an idea, or something. You never know." She turned around contentedly to the front, ready for action.

"Okay," Mike said, "we're off."

Only the problem was, they weren't. Even with all of them pushing so hard that they were making involuntary grunting noises, the bike barely moved.

"Whoa, dudes, this is gonna be *work*!" Mike said, putting words to their collective thoughts. "We're gonna have a time of it just gettin' out of the parkin' lot."

For a fraction of a second, Pam looked worried. But she shook her head quickly as if to shake off any doubts. "It's just the gravel," she shouted confidently. "Once out on the road, we'll be fine!"

But the surrey seemed to be losing its battle with the gravel. Even with all of their combined exertion, the bike only inched pathetically toward the exit in jerking movements. "Push, push," Pam shouted. "We're almost there!" she added triumphantly.

Mike, already red in the face, looked at her and shook his head. At the exit, both he and Pam yelled "Left!" and they all pushed while Mike and Pam yanked on their steering wheels.

The bike fared a bit better on the smooth surface of the road, but it was still a tremendous effort just to get it to limp along.

Every one of them must have hoped that when they got to the intersection they would have a chance to rest, because when they finally got there and the light turned green, they all groaned.

"Come on guys," Pam yelled, "turn right, and *push*!"

"Okay, dude, okay," Mike said, out of breath. "We all get the idea."

They turned right onto Lafayette street and began their slow crawl. Unfortunately, because the street was narrow, there were only two possible lanes of traffic, one each way. This meant that the bike occupied a regular car lane with no space at all to pull over. And no matter how normal the sight of a surrey was on the streets of Cape May, most driver's didn't like this arrangement one bit, and expressed that opinion with loud blows from their horns.

This occasion was no exception. No sooner had they made their turn, than the light changed again, and traffic was hard on their heels.

The car behind them crept close to the back of the bike, making everyone in the back seat nervous, and after only a few seconds the driver let his displeasure at their pace be known with a loud, sustained blow on his horn.

"O-*kay*!" They all shouted, and pushed harder yet.

But Maddy's feet kept slipping off the pedals, and Aunt Caroline's feet couldn't even reach them anyway.

As the driver of the car behind them leaned on his horn, others behind him joined in. Soon, the surrey, creeping along at a snail's pace, was leading an impatient line of honking, tooting cars, with Mike and the girls shouting angrily back.

Finally, the lane of oncoming traffic opened up, and the car behind them swerved violently around them. As it did, they all shouted "Shut up!" at the top of their lungs, and yelled at every other car in the train of angry vehicles that followed the first.

"Idiot!" shouted Zara at the last one to pass. She was red in the face and looked like she was about to explode. "I thought this would move as fast as a regular bike!"

"How can it?" shouted Pam. "There's the weight of five people!"

"Well, you should have told us this would be dangerous. Can't we get off this main road?"

"The only way to get off the main road is to ride *on* them toward the other ones," Pam sputtered. "Now *push*!"

The surrey encountered a slight decline in the road, so that they came up to the intersection with a bit less effort than before. But again, as soon as they arrived at the light, it turned green, and this time there was an eruption of cries.

Over the din, Mike could be heard shouting

directions. "Left! Left! Left onto Jackson and then right onto Mansion!" and Pam could be heard yelling "Push!" and everyone else could simply be heard yelling.

When the bike finally made it onto Mansion street, a small lane with virtually no traffic, they all stopped, panting and utterly exhausted. Mike slumped over the steering wheel, beads of perspiration dripping off of his face, and everyone in the back was wide-eyed and tomato red.

Suddenly, Zara let out an ear piercing scream. Everyone turned to look at her.

"This is *stupid*! I *hate* you, I hate *all* of you!"

But everyone was so exhausted from their effort that no one had any reaction except Maddy, who suddenly let out peels of laughter. She laughed so hard, tears streamed from her eyes. She doubled over, straightened up again, and was completely incapable of explaining herself, even though she looked like she was trying.

Finally, gasping for air, she sputtered, "I just suddenly thought that we were like one giant red turtle, taking up a whole lane of traffic," at which she lost control again, and positively howled with laughter.

Mike finally straightened up, and wiped his face with his arm. He turned to Pam.

"Well, Dude?"

Pam, beat red, didn't hesitate. "We go forward,"

she said firmly, not daring to look over her shoulder at the others.

Without even speaking, as if they were all silently resigned to following through with their original plan no matter what they really thought about it, they all started pedaling again. The surrey moved along slowly on this quiet road, aptly named Mansion Street because of the size of the Victorian homes on one side. On their left was the back of the shops that formed the Washington Street Mall, a three-block outdoor mall where no cars were allowed.

At the next stop sign, where they had arrived without too much effort, they hung a left onto Perry street, which would take them right onto Beach Drive. The only problem was, a little way down the street, the road would begin to go sharply downhill. None of the riders in the back seat knew this, of course, but Mike and Pam were familiar with the streets of their town, and when they realized what was coming up, their eyes widened--Pam's in fear, and Mike's in alarm.

Mike uttered an expletive under his breath.

"Why, what happened?" Maddy asked from the back.

"Guys," Mike threw over his shoulder, "you are going to have to get ready to brake, now, and brake *hard*."

"*What?*" Maddy asked in disbelief. But as soon as she said it, comprehension dawned. They were on crest of the slope.

"Whoa! Oh my. . .Ahhhhhhh! Ahhhhhhhh! Ahhhhhhhh! Came from behind as the bike started moving rapidly down the street. If they didn't get the bike under control, they would not only run right through the stop light at the busy intersection at the bottom of the hill, they'd crash into the concrete walkway on the opposite side that formed the "boardwalk" in Cape May.

They all knew this just by looking at what was ahead, and terror made them all attack the brakes with everything they had.

But the bike still flew down the hill, accompanied by a chorus of shrieks. As they neared the light still flying, Mike shouted, "*Right*, *Right!*" And he and Pam yanked desperately on their steering wheels.

The car at the bottom of the hill must have seen them coming, for even though it had the green light, it paused. The surrey flew toward the intersection, and made an incredibly wide right turn at the last second almost into the oncoming traffic. But all of the cars had paused on the road, as if just waiting for the impending catastrophe.

But it didn't happen. The surrey straightened out, slowed down, and pulled over.

Breathless this time from relief, no one said anything for the longest time. Finally, the silence was interrupted by Zara.

She was sputtering with pent up fury. "If I had my cell phone right now, I'd. . .I'd. . ." she paused, as if too outraged for words.

"You'd what?" Maddy challenged her. "Who would you call? Your Aunt is *here*, and the maid is probably at the beach."

Pam saw the look Zara shot Maddy, and wondered for the umpteenth time why these two even bothered with each other.

"The *beach*!" Mike moaned, his head still resting on the steering wheel. "Dudes, that's where *we* should be!"

"Nonsense!" Pam retorted. "If you weren't here with us, you'd be at the house chipping paint or something."

But as she spoke, a group of boys in long shorts crossed the street in front of them, each one carrying a surf board. Mike's eyes followed them longingly.

"Dude, you have no heart. No heart."

Pam frowned, and decided to ignore him. "Let's go. We've gone this far, there's no sense quitting now."

Mike turned around to the others in the back. "See what I mean? No heart."

Maddy giggled, Aunt Caroline blinked, and Zara ignored him. They went on their way.

Beach Drive was a wide, flat street, with enough room for the surrey to keep as far to the right as possible, out of the way of impatient drivers, and so the group pedaled leisurely for the first time since they had rented the bike.

As they headed south, the cars and pedestrians grew less in number, and the hush usual to the shore became more pronounced. Instead of traffic sounds, they heard the waves crashing to the shore and the occasional squawk of seagulls overhead. It was a hot day, but the canopy provided excellent shade, and finally their experience seemed, despite their struggles with the bike and their near disaster, like a normal outing.

They worked their way down the street in silence, each preoccupied with their own thoughts. Occasionally, Pam would point out something of interest, but Beach Drive didn't hold that many attractions. It was all hotels and restaurants.

Finally, they came to a halt at a dead-end. A metal road block terminated the street abruptly, beyond which a stretch of sandy beach undulated far into the distance.

"*That's* where South Cape May used to be," pronounced Pam.

They all climbed shakily off the bike. Aunt Caroline walked unsteadily over to a large rock, and sat down.

"Are you okay?" Pam asked.

Aunt Caroline just looked up, blinked and nodded slightly.

Pam resumed her lecture. "This road ran straight

down to that lighthouse way over there." She pointed at something that looked more than a mile away. "I used to think that South Cape May was out that way," she pointed out over the water, "but from those pictures in that book, the road went straight on through. So basically, that's where your house used to be."

The area she was referring to was half ocean, half beach. Water and land came together in a large crescent about a mile long. The water was so calm, surfing would have been pointless. Back behind the beach on the right rose high sand dunes behind which they could see nothing but waving grasses.

"What's over there?" Maddy asked, pointing to the right, behind the dunes.

"A nature sanctuary. It goes way back, and then over toward the lighthouse."

Zara stood at the metal rails, looking over the scene. "Well, Aunt Caroline," she sniffed, "this is where our whole summer house used to be," as if that were not exactly to its credit.

Aunt Caroline still sat on the rock, blinking.

Pam, knowing that there was nothing else to see, said, "Let's go. Let's ride around in West Cape May, and look at houses. Maybe we'll see something that looks like yours."

"But Dude, our hour's nearly up!" Mike protested.

"So? We'll just pay more. Our job's not done."

"Phew," Mike said, clearly exasperated. "And to think I thought I was gettin' some time off today."

They all got back on the bike rather reluctantly, but no one objected out loud.

They maneuvered the bike around, and headed back up the street. This time, the beach was on their right.

"We'll be turning left on Broadway. It's two streets up," Pam announced.

They pedaled forward. But as the surrey neared that intersection, Pam's mouth dropped open in astonishment. She pointed, dumbfounded, at a girl riding toward them on a bright green bike with a yellow basket.

"What, what is it?" Maddy asked.

"My bike! My bike! It's *her*. . .and. . . my *bike*. . . let's go! Let's *go*!" She practically pounded on the steering wheel.

They all had some idea by this time what she was talking about, and so they watched the girl on the bike with interest as she came toward the intersection, then smoothly coasted right onto Broadway, the road they were just getting ready to take.

"Come *on*!" Pam insisted. So instead of resuming their leisurely ride, they once again found themselves pushing against the pedals with all their might, all in order to catch up with the young rider on the green bike.

"*Push! Push!*" Pam yelled.

"Dude, give us all a break and join the army!"

But Pam's only response was "*Push!*"

To which Zara yelled, breathless but full of loathing, "I *am* pushing, and I *hate* you!"

But Pam didn't respond. Here she was, within a few feet of her own bike and the thief who stole it, and she wasn't about to let either of them out of her sight. She was going to have it out with the girl once and for all, and bring that bike home like a trophy.

The girl turned a corner, and the surrey followed close behind.

Chapter Fifteen

"**D**on't take your eyes off of her!" Pam yelled. The others simply panted in response. From the back, between gasps of breath, Maddy shouted,

"What. . .are you going. . .to do. . .when. . .you catch up to her?"

Pam turned around with a frown, and gasped back, "I'll worry. . .about that. . .*later*!"

But while Pam had had her head turned, the girl on the bike, who had all the while been increasing her distance from them, suddenly turned.

"Oh no!" Pam wailed. "She's gone! I missed it! It's all your fault!"

"At the yellow house," Maddy sputtered through giggles. "Left at the yellow house!" And then she gave way to another fit of giggles as her feet slipped off the pedals yet again.

"What the heck are you laughing at?" Pam yelled, annoyed.

"You!" Both Maddy and Mike shouted in unison.

"Oh brother! Now *push*!" she cried, as the surrey turned recklessly at the yellow house.

They were now riding on what looked like a picture-perfect country lane. All of the bustling town life of hotels and motels, shops and restaurants, although only a few blocks away, seemed to have been left far, far behind, a part of another world. Instead, they found themselves immersed in the deep silence of the countryside, the only sound that of the rustling grasses in the meadow.

Finally, after a fairly long stretch of smooth road on which they had actually gotten closer to her, the girl on the bike turned right, and the surrey followed her onto an even smaller and more remote country lane. Except for when the girl had ridden right by her on the street, this was the closest Pam had ever been to her. Now, as they got closer, Pam finally started to get nervous about the confrontation, and wondered what she'd actually say. Her stomach churned.

Just then, something caught her eye, and she turned her head to look at it more fully.

"Come on Dude, stay with us. We're almost there. But there'd better not be any bloodshed," Mike warned her.

Pam's attention came back to the bike in front of her, whose rider was now coming to a halt.

The girl stopped in front of one of the most ramshackle dwellings Pam had ever seen. It looked exactly like one of those houses in the picture books of Cape

May storms, *after* the storm had hit. The two-story wooden dwelling actually tilted to one side. The porch roof sagged in the middle, and the rickety looking steps leading onto the porch looked like they hadn't been used in years.

"This is where she *lives?*" Maddy gasped, incredulous.

"Dude, I don't know. Maybe you should back off. There might be wild dogs in there or something," Mike offered by way of helpful advice.

The surrey came to a stop. At the sound, the girl looked up, surprised. The group in the surrey was out of breath, red in the face, and looked every bit as if they'd been following her. Suddenly, Pam realized how bizarre the whole thing was, and just sat there, gaping. All sensation had drained from her legs.

As the girl just stood there at the rickety gate looking at them, a feeling of awkwardness fell over the whole group. Even Maddy didn't look in the least disposed to giggle.

Then, as if there was nothing unusual about the scene, the girl simply turned away, and started to open the gate.

A feeling of outrage swept over Pam, and a fierce mobility came back to her. She jumped down from the surrey, and strode over to the girl just as she was getting ready to pass through the gate with the bike.

"Hey, what do you think you're doing?" was all Pam could think of for an opening move.

"What?" the girl responded, surprised.

"What do you think you're doing? With that bike?" Pam asked, angry with the girl's apparent incomprehension. "*My* bike!" she added, as if that would clear everything up.

A strange look came over the other girl's face, and she clutched at the handlebars of the bike.

"No. This is my bike."

"No it *isn't*," Pam said assertively. "It's mine, and you stole it! Right out of my driveway. And I want it back."

"Dude, take it easy!" Mike interjected from the surrey.

The girl's face registered surprise, fear, and dismay all at once. "Stole it?" she repeated. "This is *my* bike, my gran bought it for me. It was a present."

"No it can't be. I know my bike," Pam insisted, outraged by the girl's persistence. "My bike had the exact same color, same basket, and even those stupid little flowers." She pointed to the flowers that decorated the basket. "It even has the scratches on it from when I fell after riding down the ramp on the boardwalk. You see, right there," Pam pointed. "This is *my* bike, and I want to know why you took it."

"But I didn't!" The girl's eyes had started to well

up. "This was a present. My Christmas present. From my gran." She looked down at the scratches with a puzzled look, and then started crying in earnest, her tears trickling down her face. But she didn't wipe them away. Her small hands tightened their grip on the handlebars.

Pam was stunned. Of all the reactions she expected from the creep who stole her bike, this wasn't one of them. She whirled around to face the surrey with her hands outstretched in disbelief.

But Mike looked serious as he stared at the girl. He got down off the surrey, and came over toward Pam. "Dude, are you sure about this? I mean, this girl doesn't sound like she's lying. Maybe you got the wrong bike."

Pam slapped her sides in exasperation. "I *know* I'm right. It's the *one*. The one that was stolen from me last fall."

"I didn't get this bike till Christmas," the girl sobbed. "It was my present. My *only* present."

"Oh brother!" was all Pam said. Mike shifted uncomfortably. Everything became still and quiet, as Pam hesitated, certain she was correct, but frustrated that now she seemed to be losing ground. Weird, too, was the girl's reaction. There was no defiance, no challenge, nothing.

Frustrated, Pam suddenly said, "I'm just going to call the police."

That caused an uproar. Objections rang out from everywhere, even from the surrey behind her. Mike took her to task rather bluntly for being too harsh, while the girl started almost choking with sobs.

"So what do I do?" Pam asked impatiently.

"Let it go, dude, let it go," Mike said, sounding like he'd had enough of the whole thing. "You can get another bike."

"*What?*" Pam exploded. Thoughts of all that she'd missed out on so far that summer because of not having her bike, and thoughts of everything she'd put up with at the *Chocolate Pot* in order to get another one all crowded together, making her speechless with fury.

All of a sudden, a sharp, strident voice barked from one of the shack's upstairs windows.

"*What's going on down there?*"

The little girl cringed. She raised blank and fearful eyes up toward the direction of the voice, but seemed unable to speak. Then, a back door slammed. None of them, including Mike, looked too happy at the prospect of meeting the owner of that voice face to face. But instead, an old woman rounded the corner of the house, moving rapidly toward them.

The little girl looked so relieved, she started quietly sobbing again.

"What's going on here?" the old woman asked, firmly but quietly, almost in a whisper.

"They're trying to take my bike," the little girl said tearfully.

Exasperated at the other girl's insistence, Pam explained the situation to the old woman, her voice carrying loudly through the silence.

Suddenly, the man's voice intruded from the upstairs window once more, this time screaming in fury.

"*I said, what's going on down there?*"

Both the old woman and the little girl cringed, and looked a silent accusation at the group.

"*Keep it down, will you?*" the old woman said in a hard whisper, while the little girl started to quake. "I'll tell you where I got this bike. I got it at the local police auction for the borough. They're always havin' auctions of stuff they gather up throughout the year. This bike was probably abandoned by whoever took it, the police got a hold of it, and sold it for auction. And that's that." She put her hands on her hips.

Mike shuffled his feet, and turned to Pam. "Dude, that makes sense. The cops do that. It's perfectly legit. It's also legit to buy 'em that way.

Pam was experiencing that crackling sensation in the back of her throat which only meant one thing. Tears were on their way. She turned away in frustration so that no one would see them.

But the old woman must have known. "I paid ten dollars for this bike at the auction. Let's say we split that. You give me five dollars, and I"ll let you have the bike back."

At this, the little girl let out a howl audible far above the whispers in which they'd all been speaking.

The old woman rounded on her violently. "*Sshh*! You want *him* coming down?"

The little girl shook her head and sobbed silently, her fingers still gripping the handlebars.

"Well, Dude, whatdya say?"

Pam looked at the sobbing girl, whose misery was almost unbearable to watch. She looked around at the overgrown yard, at the shabby, falling-down house, and thought of what it must be like to live in there. She thought also of what the owner of that voice must be like, to have these two people cowering in fear at it. And suddenly Pam knew that she could never pry the bike from the other girl's fingers. She knew, without thinking it through clearly, that it would be far worse for the other girl than it was for her when it was stolen last fall.

But she couldn't say all of this. She didn't know how.

"Nah, that's okay." She swallowed hard. "After all, I might be wrong, and. . .and. . ."

"And that wouldn't be cool," Mike finished for her.

Pam just shook her head, and they both turned back toward the surrey.

Chapter Sixteen

When they were all settled on the bike once again, and turning it around to head back, Mike patted Pam on the shoulder.

"Ya did right, ya know. I'm proud of ya."

Pam didn't have a chance to respond because Maddy immediately pounded her with questions.

"So, what did they say? Are you just going to let her keep it? I don't get it. Wasn't it yours after all?"

Pam stared straight ahead, incapable of answering, so Mike answered for her. He explained the entire situation, finishing up with, "And ya know what Dude? It was noble. Downright noble. I'm really proud of ya."

Pam squirmed in embarrassment.

"Now Dudes, we've got to get this bike back to the shop. We're already twenty minutes late. How's everybody doin' back there, anyway?"

Mike turned around to the back seat. Maddy looked as animated as ever, Zara as stony as ever, with a deep crease between her brows, and Aunt Caroline had fallen asleep.

Satisfied that everything was normal, Mike turned

back around and said, "We'll get back in no time, guys. Just pedal steadily, and take it easy."

There were no objections to that, not even from Pam, who was lost in thought. So the surrey started off slowly, ambling leisurely back down the country lane.

Suddenly, Pam swung her head around to look at something they'd just passed.

"Dude, what's up with the garage? You know someone there?"

Sure enough, it was a mechanic's shop that had caught Pam's eye, full of cars in the wide driveway where a man was tinkering under an open hood.

She peered intently until the surrey made a left, and the garage was out of sight. She glanced at everyone in the back seat. No one had noticed anything.

Pam felt a flip-flop of excitement in her stomach. She was positive about what she had seen.

But now was not the time to divulge her suspicions. They were all too tired for another adventure, and they were late with the bike, anyway. She'd wait until she could talk it over with Maddy. No sense getting Aunt Caroline all excited for nothing, because her suspicions could, after all, turn out to be wrong. But that possibility didn't dampen her enthusiasm in the least. She knew she was onto something. At the thought, she felt another exhilarating wave of excitement. She simply couldn't wait to talk about it to Maddy.

"So Dude," Mike began, interrupting her reverie, "what time do you have to be at work?"

"What!!!" Pam shouted. "Oh *brother*!" A feeling of dread completely displaced her current excitement.

Maddy started to giggle.

"What? What's up?" Mike asked.

"Nothing!" Pam said firmly, daring anyone to contradict her. Maddy's giggles simply increased.

Mike looked sideways at Pam, and shrugged his shoulders, apparently deciding to let it go.

They rode on in silence, gradually leaving the countryside behind them, along with the mingled smell of hay and honeysuckle, which would soon be replaced by the scent of salty air mixed with coconut oil.

It was now a beautiful afternoon, a bit cooler than when they'd started out, with a delicate breeze rippling the edges of the canopy.

But for Pam, it could have snowed right then and there and she wouldn't have been distracted from the dread she felt at the prospect now looming before her of telling her parents she'd been fired.

But she would have to do it. There was no way around it. Fleeting thoughts of skipping off to the boardwalk at six o'clock and simply whiling away two hours crossed her mind. But the thought of deceiving her parents like that made her feel even worse. So she sighed loudly and resigned herself to a full confession.

The surrey turned right at Broadway which would take them back up to Beach Drive. Mike had decided that they would take the flattest route home, but even so, he reminded them, they were going to be extremely late. Not to mention the fact that they'd owe more money on the bike.

"Do we *have* more money?" Pam asked everyone in general, digging into her pockets.

"I don't think I have enough," Mike said. "Dude, I think we're going to have to swing by your house and get some cash. That way," he said over his should to Zara, "you and your aunt can just go home."

"Thank God!" was Zara's response.

In the meantime, Aunt Caroline had finally woken up, and Maddy was filling her in on their escapade. When the old woman finally grasped the story of the stolen bike, she blinked a few times and said, "But what about the house? Did we find anything?"

Maddy giggled. "I think we got a little distracted from what we went out for in the first place!"

"I'll say!" Zara said crossly.

Aunt Caroline tried not to look too disappointed, while Pam looked straight ahead, saying nothing.

They made a turn, and then another, and before long, they were on their own street. These houses were such a contrast to what they had just seen, with lush green grass smooth and velvety looking, and everything clean and neat.

Suddenly, Maddy cried out, "Zara, you have another car in your driveway!"

Zara and Aunt Caroline leaned forward to look down the drive, where, sure enough, another shiny black Mercedes was parked just behind the one that had brought both of them to the shore.

"*Oh no*!" Zara and Aunt Caroline cried simultaneously, looking aghast.

"What? What is it?" Pam asked, extremely curious.

But the two in the back were silent and staring, identical expressions of dismay on both of their faces.

As Mike jumped down off the surrey and ran into the Fischer's house, Maddy explained with a sigh, "That car belongs to Zara's grandmother, you know, Aunt Caroline's sister.

"So?" Pam said, uncomprehending.

As if right on cue to explain what the big deal was, a very tall, grey-haired woman exploded out the front door, leaving the screen door to bang behind her.

It seemed as if both Zara and her aunt quaked at the sight, and both appeared to be extremely reluctant to get out of the surrey.

"Caroline! Caroline! What have you been up to? Get out of that silly contraption, and help me get settled in here."

The tall woman trumpeted her command across the yard with the confidence of an army sergeant expecting immediate compliance.

Suddenly, Zara and her aunt found new energy. They hastened off the bike, and scurried across the yard toward the house. Pam just stared. She hadn't thought that Zara was capable of such submission, or that Aunt Caroline was capable of moving so fast.

"*That's* the *grandmother?*" she asked Maddy incredulously, wondering how come she'd never seen her before, living right next door as she did. "Oh *brother!*"

Just then Mike climbed back into the surrey and said, "Okay, Dudes, we've got to get this back. No lollygagging around. That guy'll have the cops on us if we don't hurry."

As they pulled away, Zara's grandmother could still be heard inside the house bellowing orders. "Whew! Better her than me," Pam said aloud, thinking that she'd had enough of mean old women barking orders for the summer.

Then she remembered something. "Will you come by tomorrow?" she said over her shoulder to Maddy. "Alone, I mean?"

Maddy shrugged, and said "Sure. But why not tonight?"

"Uh, well," Pam began, looking sideways at Mike, "I have to spend some time with my parents, remember?" she said meaningfully.

Maddy giggled. Mike said, "And don't forget to tell them how noble you were, dude. Really. Don't forget. It's okay to pat yourself on the back once in a while."

Pam squirmed. "Yeah, right."

Chapter Seventeen

Pam entered the back door of her house, and saw that her parents were preparing dinner. It was quiet in the kitchen, so without making a sound, Pam slid into her seat by the window, her stomach churning with both anxiety and hunger. It had been hours since she'd eaten, and she was positively starving. But what if they were so mad at her they sent her to bed without supper? At the thought, Pam let out an involuntary groan.

Her mother whirled around.

"Pam! I didn't hear you come in!" Then, glancing at her watch she said, "You're late. Aren't you supposed to be at *The Chocolate Pot?*"

Pam groaned again, and put her head down into her plate. It was agony. They were going to be so disappointed, if not furious, especially considering how much she had begged them to let her take on Katy's job. She groaned once more.

"Pam?" Her father's voice sounded sharper than usual. Oh *brother*, she thought. It was going to be bad, so there was no point in delaying. Her stomach rumbled in agreement.

"I'm not going back," was the muffled reply into the plate.

"What?" her mother asked, pausing in her preparations and looking directly at her. "Did you say you're not going back?"

Pam nodded, her forehead still glued to the china plate.

"What do you mean?"

"It means I'm not going back!" Pam said a little louder, still into the plate.

"Pam, pick your head up and answer your mother," Mr. Fischer said crisply. Clearly, Pam wasn't the only one who'd had a long and tiring day, because both of her parents seemed a bit more short tempered than usual.

"I did answer her," Pam said crossly, lifting her head up reluctantly. "I said I'm not going back!" She tried to look at her father, who was peering at her over the rim of his glasses, but she squirmed under the steadiness of his gaze. She looked instead at her mother, who had finished putting bread in a basket and now had her hands on her hips, her attention focused entirely on her daughter.

Pam swallowed hard, and plunged in. "I was fired." At that, her forehead once again found her plate.

"*What??*" the Fischers said in unison.

"Yep. I was *fired*. *She* fired me. The old *biddy* fired me."

"Why? What happened?" Mrs. Fischer asked, sounding genuinely confused. "Everything was going so well!" At that, Pam snorted.

"Are you sure? I mean, what exactly did she say?"

"She said, 'You're *fired!*' Only at the top of her lungs so that the whole boardwalk could hear. Believe me, I'm fired."

Mrs. Fischer looked as if she didn't know what to say next, and looked to her husband. Mr. Fischer was silent, but the side of his mouth twitched.

"Pam," he said, "tell us exactly what happened."

So she related the events that had brought about her rather abrupt release from *The Chocolate Pot*. Although in the past few weeks she had regaled her parents with stories about the old woman's treatment of her, she had never before told them with such conviction. But although both of them listened carefully to Pam's tale of mistreatment, her father still saw it from an employer's point of view.

"Are you saying that you were standing there, talking with your friends, while you were supposed to be working?"

"Well, I guess you could say that. But it wasn't for long. And besides, Maddy had something to tell me. But I *swear*, it wasn't for long!"

Her mother made a sympathetic sound. Her father looked thoughtful. Mrs. Fischer, looking at her husband, said, "Shall we call the store and talk to her, or call Bob and ask to meet with both of them?"

At this, Pam snorted. "Yeah, and while you're talking, why don't you ask her who she is, and what the heck her name is."

Mr. Fischer's mouth twitched again.

Her mother frowned, and said, "Seriously, Pam, do you want us to help you get your job back? Won't you be leaving Katy in a difficult spot if you don't fulfill your promise?"

Pam hadn't even considered the possibility that they might try and help her get her job back. The only thing that she had thought about the entire day was her dread of this conversation. The possibility of even being *able* to go back to the candy store never even occurred to her. And she definitely did not like the idea. In fact, the idea of going back made her sicker than she'd felt all day.

"No!" she exploded. "No! No *way*! I *hate* it there. You don't know what it was like, with that old woman picking on me the whole time. *No!*" she repeated, shaking her head violently, "I don't want it back! I'll just have to come clean with Katy and explain how horrible it was."

"Are you sure it isn't worth it?" her father asked. "After all, how are you going to get another bike? It's a little late in the summer to pick up another summer job."

"But I found it!" Pam perked up, considerably more excited. "I found my bike!" And so, as her parents resumed dinner preparations, and finally, put it all out on the table, Pam related that day's adventures on the surrey. Her father raised his eyebrows when she described the moment they all decided to chase after the girl on the stolen bike, and her mother looked positively bewildered.

But when she described her confrontation with the girl, and her decision to let the bike go, both of her parents looked positively amazed. Mr. Fischer put his napkin down, took his glasses off, and said, "Pam, I am proud of you. *Very* proud. You really did the right thing. You had a choice to insist on your right to the bike, or to be generous, and you chose to be generous. I'm glad."

Pam beamed at her father's praise. But her mother looked like something was still nagging at her. "But why did the police auction it off? I mean we went to them as soon as it was stolen."

"Because we went to Cape May City police. Whoever stole it must have dropped it off in West Cape May, and *their* police found it. And I guess there just isn't that much communication between the two police units."

"Oh *brother*," was all Pam's mother said.

"Anyway," Pam's father continued, "this means you

still don't have a bike, and now have no means of saving for one. What about that?"

Pam thought for a minute. "I think I'm more interested in this mystery of Aunt Caroline's right now. I'd like a bike, but what I'd really like is to see if I'm right about my idea."

And so Pam began to relate the other part of her adventure, the one she hadn't told anyone else about. And her parents listened, thoroughly intrigued by her hunch.

Later that evening, when Pam was upstairs in her room, dressed in her pajamas and nestled amid fluffy pillows, thinking that finally, all was right with the world again, there came a knock at the door.

"Come in," she said, thinking it must be one of her parents.

But it was Maddy who entered, looking bathed and refreshed. She was carrying a rather large, hardcover book. Pam eyed it with suspicion.

"I know you said to come by tomorrow, but I thought you might like this," she said, indicating the book. "I asked my mom if I could lend you my first *Harry Potter*, and she said it would be okay. So here it is," Maddy said enthusiastically, handing Pam her treasure with several shrugs of her shoulders. Then, bouncing up onto Pam's four-poster, she made herself right at home.

Pam looked at the book with dismay, but managed a polite thank-you. "But why do you have this? I mean, down here, with you, on vacation?"

"Oh," Maddy nodded vigorously, "I never go anywhere without some of my library. I always bring at least ten of my favorites."

"*Ten?*"

"Uh huh. It's always so hard to choose. But you've got to get started on it," she said, patting the book and continuing to bounce up and down. "That way, we'll be able to talk about it."

Pam viewed that prospect with considerably less enthusiasm.

"I was also extremely curious about the thing you wanted to tell me. In fact, I'm *very* curious," she said, nodding vigorously.

At this Pam laughed. "Well, I don't want to disappoint you. I mean, I don't know if it's going to turn out to be anything important, but I think I saw a building that might be the one that used to be attached to the house next door."

"*What???*" Maddy screamed.

"Shhhh. Keep it down. This is an inn, remember?"

But Maddy hardly heard Pam's reproach. She was beside herself with excitement. The bed was now undulating like a rough sea. "What? Where? Why didn't you *say* something?"

"Because," Pam tried to explain calmly, "I was focused on the bike in front of us–my stolen bike, re- member?–and I only glanced at the building. Something caught my eye, but I was too distracted to really think about it. Then, on the way back, when we were going slowly along that road, I looked at it more carefully. It was then," she continued with satisfaction, "that I knew what had struck me. The building–it's a garage or something–has dormer windows just like the house next door, with criss-crossing panes and everything."

Pam paused. Maddy's bounces were slowing down. "That's *it*? Dormer windows? Criss-crossing panes? What's the big deal? Your house has dormer windows." Her head nodded in the direction of Pam's own bedroom windows. "My house at home has dor- mer windows. So what?"

"Look. The ones on Aunt Caroline's house are very rare. For a Victorian house, that is. I know. I look at houses. I've grown up here. And I've been inside tons. It's unusual in a Victorian house to have attic dormer windows that are narrow with criss-crossing panes that make a diamond pattern. I thought about that when I was up in that attic with you guys, trying to open those windows. I guess that just stuck in my head."

Maddy still looked doubtful.

"Yes, I see." She paused for a while to think. Then she giggled. "How do you know all this stuff?"

Pam shrugged. It's just like you and horses. You know a lot about them because they're your hobby, you ride them all the time, and you take lessons. Well, houses are my hobby. And, living with my mother, believe me, it's like those riding lessons."

Maddy nodded at this, and ran her eyes over Pam's model house that sat on the table before the window. "Yeah, I guess that makes sense. But what now? How do we find out for sure?"

"We have to go back. Only this time, it should be just the two of us. We need to be able to take our time, and really look it over. And hopefully, find something else that will be more convincing."

"Were going to have to go onto someone's property?" Maddy asked.

"Of course," Pam said shortly, pulling her covers up around her. "How else?"

"Hm. Well, I have to go. I'll see you tomorrow.

"Okay, see you."

Maddy bounced one last time, right off the bed, and was out the door in a flash. Pam looked down at the book she had left behind. *Harry Potter and the Sorcerer's Stone*. She sighed, and, reluctantly picking up the heavy book, turned to the first page.

Chapter Eighteen

Morning light was streaming through the dormer windows of Pam's bedroom. Mrs. Fischer came in quietly and gently shook her daughter. She raised her eyebrows when she saw that a book had fallen beside the sleeping girl, and, picking it up with curiosity, she set it on the night stand. She also switched off the lamp that sat in its center. At the sound, Pam woke up and rubbed her eyes.

"Breakfast," was all her mom said, and she left the room.

Pam gazed around her sleepily, wondering why she hadn't woken up sooner. Her stomach was growling in impatience. Then her eyes fell on the book that her mom had just placed on the night stand. "Oh *brother*," she said aloud.

She reluctantly got out of bed, hating to leave its plump comforts behind. But the scent of breakfast beckoned, and soon enough, she was dressed and scurrying downstairs. All thoughts of investigating houses took a backseat to her interest in what lay on the breakfast table.

It wasn't until she was in the middle of chores, working on those wretched roses that lined the front, that she thought once again about the garage. She considered asking her mom for the money to rent bikes to go back to West Cape May, but after last night, and how understanding her parents had been, Pam felt reluctant. After all, she'd been lucky to get off with no scolding or punishment. Why push it?

But then, how on earth could she get back to that garage? It was way too far to walk. A couple of miles in fact. More than halfway from her house to the lighthouse.

Just then, Maddy bounded up.

"Boy, you sure are always working," she said, head nodding vigorously up and down at this extraordinary fact.

That was Maddy—always stating the incredibly obvious.

She plopped down next to Pam and said, "I don't know why you're always complaining about your chores. Your garden is *be-oo-tiful*." She was looking around, taking in the whole picture.

"Yeah, but *these*. What do you think of *these*," Pam said, pointing to the sorry looking sticks that had but a handful of roses blooming on them.

Maddy tilted her head, looking as if she were trying to find something tactful to say.

"Well," she said nodding vigorously, "they could use a few more flowers."

"You think?"

"Uh huh," Maddy responded with several nods, oblivious to Pam's sarcasm. "So, when are we going back to that garage that you saw? And how are we going to get there?"

"I'm not sure. I haven't figured that out yet. But after I finish up here, let's meet up, and I'll show you on *that* house," she pointed next door, "what I'm talking about."

"Okeydoke," Maddy said, getting to her feet. "When should I come back?"

"I need another half hour for this, and fifteen minutes to get cleaned up."

"Right. An hour then." Maddy skipped off.

"Three-quarters!" Pam shouted after her.

At precisely three quarters of an hour later, Pam was sitting on the back steps of her house, freshly scrubbed. As soon as Maddy appeared, Pam stood up and motioned for her to follow. She led the other girl down the Fischer's driveway toward the street, and then turned right at the sidewalk. She walked to the spot directly in front of Aunt Caroline's house, and then backed out into the street.

"Come on," she said, gesturing to Maddy, "you

can't see from the sidewalk. You have to stand back."

As soon as the two girls had positioned themselves in the street, Pam pointed up to the top of the house and said, "It's hard to see through the leaves, but what do you see?"

Maddy tilted her head to one side, then to the other, shrugged, and said sheepishly, "I have no idea. The roof? I can't see the cupola from here."

"No. Look at the windows. Can you see them? Can you see anything about them?"

"Yes, they're the dormer windows we opened when we went up into the attic. But I still can't see what's so special about them."

Pam put her hands on Maddy's shoulders, and turned her around to view a street full of Victorian houses of all different shapes and sizes.

"Look around at the rest of the houses. At the roofs. What do you see that's different?"

Maddy looked at the houses on the street with a blank expression. She stared long and hard at the roofs, and at all the different styles of dormer windows, certain that the other girl was seeing something she wasn't. She then turned back to Aunt Caroline's house, and peered intently at the dormer windows on the roof. Her expression changed.

"Okay. You're right. Most of the dormer windows on this block have square panes in them, and on Aunt

Caroline's house, the panes are diamond shaped. I see it. But so what?"

"Just get exactly what they look like into your head."

Maddy shrugged, and obligingly stared up at the roof again, intent on getting a clear mental picture of what she was seeing.

Just then, the front door of Aunt Caroline's house opened, and the older of the two sisters emerged. Once again, Pam was struck by the huge difference between Aunt Caroline and her older sister. No two related people could have appeared more dissimilar. Aunt Caroline reminded her of a cute, tiny, winking fairy with white cotton candy hair, who, if she had a chance, would wave her wand and grant you your greatest wish. But her older sister seemed more like every kid's idea of what a mean school principal would look like, or more importantly, sound like, just at the moment they were telling you that you had to take summer school, or had half a year's detention, or some such similar fate.

And she was barreling down on them like she meant business. Pam and Maddy looked at each other in alarm.

"You!" The barreling force thundered, pointing directly at Pam. "You!" The voice thundered again as it swiftly crossed the lawn. Pam and Maddy both backed even further into the street.

"You!" A finger was now inches from Pam's face. "You're the upstart who's stirring up trouble around here. Why?"

Trouble? Pam wondered for a second if this crazy woman hadn't mistaken her for some other unlucky kid.

"No. . .I. . .what are you . . .I think you must. . ." she stammered.

"What are you encouraging that bubble-headed sister of mine for? Can't you see she's crackers? Anyone but a complete dope could see that! What are you, a complete dope? Now quit this nonsense! There's no treasure, and that's that! Not in this house anyway. You want treasure?" The finger shifted direction, and pointed up the street. "Go up to the beach and start digging!" And suddenly, the tall, steel-gray woman turned on her heel and strode forcefully back into the house and slammed the door.

Maddy started giggling uncontrollably. Pam's mouth was open, but no sound came out. But if she *had* made any sound, laughter wouldn't have been it. She was outraged.

Did she hear that right? Did that crazy, mean gray giant actually call Aunt Caroline *crackers*? Her own sister? And did she actually call me a *dope*? Pam thought to herself. A *dope*?

Pam was stunned. Her brain reeled. Fury swept through her.

It was horrible enough to hear Aunt Caroline insulted like that. She may occasionally seem a little spacey, but she was one of the kindest, nicest old people Pam had ever met. To hear her insulted made Pam feel sick to her stomach. But on top of that, she had to listen to someone implying that she was stupid? After all the insults she'd put up with at *The Chocolate Pot*? It was outrageous. She'd had enough of mean, nasty old ladies for the summer. E-*nough*.

A firm resolve swept through her, and suddenly she started marching toward her house. "Stay here," she yelled over her shoulder to Maddy. "We're going to get bikes." And she stomped up the front porch stairs.

Pam bellowed for her mother from the front door, completely disregarding the fact that there were guests in the inn, possibly in want of peace and quiet. "Mom!" she bellowed again, getting closer to the kitchen.

Pam flung herself through the swing doors of the kitchen, and, before her surprised mother could say anything, launched into her demand.

"Mom, I know I was let off easy last night for being fired, but I absolutely need money to rent bikes for me and Maddy. We're going to look at that building I saw because I'm sure I'm right. It's the one, and I want Maddy to see it."

She stood there resolute. Her mother paused, taking a minute to absorb what Pam had said, and how she'd said it. Then she put down the rolling pin she was using, went over to her handbag on a kitchen chair, and pulled out some money.

"This should do it," she said simply, and turned back to her baking.

Minutes later, Pam and Maddy were trotting briskly through Cape May's tree-lined streets, and in short time they were at the center of town. The bike attendant recognized them from the day before, and, taking their money, reminded them sternly not to be late.

For the first time in many, many months, Pam experienced the exhilaration of riding again. As soon as her tires hit paved road, she leaned into the pedals with a vengeance. She kept on riding furiously, and didn't slow down until her leg muscles shook and a sharp pain shot through each thigh.

But soon she realized that she'd left Maddy way behind, so she reluctantly slowed down and then finally came to a full stop, waiting impatiently with one foot on a pedal, ready to take off again.

When Maddy caught up she grinned sheepishly at Pam, and said, gasping, "I need to slow down. I have a cramp in my side."

Pam shrugged, and said, "Whatever."

So they took it easy from there, meandering the back way through town, avoiding the beach front altogether. This was the most direct route to their destination anyway, and consequently, the girls arrived at the country portion of West Cape May in less than half the time it took the surrey the day before. The scent of hay and honeysuckle greeted them once more, wafted along gently by a welcome breeze. It was late morning, and the air still had a morning freshness to it, even though the sun beat down steadily.

They rode along lazily, made a few turns, and were soon nearing the street where the blond haired girl lived. But Pam wasn't thinking about that girl or her old bike just then. Her thoughts were entirely centered on investigating her hunch, and most importantly, proving she was right.

And so it was only just after turning onto the street where they'd been the night before, that Pam signaled Maddy to stop. She pointed to a building on their right.

"Let's pull over to the far side of the road, so we're not so obvious," Pam suggested. The building in question was clearly a mechanic's garage, with a paved double driveway and two large garage doors in the front. It sat next to a quaint little wooden Victorian house with a tiny porch decorated in chipping white paint. They could see the blond haired girl's house from where they were standing, looking, as it did yesterday, like it would fall over if you just blew hard enough.

But it was the garage that interested Pam. It was perfectly square, and unlike most garages, had a second story. It was toward the roof that Pam now pointed.

"See?" she said nudging Maddy. "Do you see anything familiar?"

"Well," Maddy said cautiously, buying time while her eyes traveled over the roof, "I see dormer windows, and . . . oh my *gosh*! They're exactly like the ones on Aunt Caroline's house! I can't believe it! I mean, *exactly*! The windows have those same diamond shaped panes! Even I can see it!" she said excitedly, hopping up and down. "The whole thing, the whole top of the house, looks like Aunt Caroline's house, only," she said tilting her head, "smaller, somehow. Shorter."

"Yes," Pam said, nodding her head, "like a smaller model. It's only two stories high, for one thing. And its narrower. It must have stuck on the back like a littler version of the main part of the house."

"Except that it has garage doors," Maddy said doubtfully, wrinkling her nose, "and it's missing the cupola, and that's the important part."

"The garage doors are no big deal," Pam said with confidence. "People change their houses all the time. And let's face it, if you can *move* a house, you can build garage doors into it. But as for the cupola, well, I just don't know. Maybe," Pam said slowly, thinking, "maybe the cupola fell off, or was taken off. We have to find out. We *have* to. We just *have* to." She paused. "But *how?*"

The two girls fell silent. The place looked completely deserted, and both girls were at a loss for their next move. But then, one of the garage doors was suddenly opened from the inside by a man in overalls. He'd obviously been hard at work, for his clothes were streaked with black marks and his hands looked dark and grimy. He stopped and looked across the street at the two girls.

Pam and Maddy quickly turned to each other as if they were deep in conversation. Pam was all for going over to the guy and asking him questions about the building. Maddy thought that was crazy, and said so. So they stood there quietly arguing about it until the guy lost interest and turned back to work.

Now that one of the garage doors was opened, it was easy to see in. It was crammed with cars, car parts, and tools, and also looked as if its ceiling went all the way up to the roof.

As Pam stood there, indecisive about whether to go across the street and talk to the man or not, she heard Maddy gasp, and say, "Look!"

It was the girl on Pam's old bike again, riding toward them. When she saw Pam and Maddy, she looked frightened, and stared hard at them as she rode by, keeping her eyes on the two girls even as she went some distance down the street. She then sped up, and swiftly got herself and the bike through the rickety gate, and around the house, out of sight.

Both girls watched her silently. Then Maddy said, "She probably thinks you want the bike back–that you've changed your mind."

Pam shrugged. "I said I didn't, and that's that. I've got other things to think about now. The question is, what do we *do*?"

She looked back over at the garage, and stood with her hands on her hips, thinking. Suddenly she turned.

"You do believe me, don't you? I mean, you do think this is it, right?"

Maddy answered carefully. "I don't know that this is it, but I do know that it looks exactly like Aunt Caroline's house, only smaller," she finished, her head bobbing up and down.

Pam looked satisfied.

"Come on, let's go. We need a grown-up this time."

Chapter Nineteen

Pam was sitting on the long, low porch swing with Maddy and Zara, slowly rocking back and forth, listening to the two elderly sisters argue.

They were really going at it. With neither of them saying anything that they hadn't already heard for years, their debate had readily descended into the childish.

"I did too!"

"You did not! Absurd!"

"I *did*, I tell you, I *did*!"

"You heard nothing of the kind. Absolute rubbish. You were too young."

"I *did* hear it! I *did*, I tell you!"

Pam yawned loudly. She grinned sheepishly as everyone turned to look at her.

Mrs. Van den Burgh turned to her sister. "There, see? All this nonsense is tiring this kid out. How you ever got the neighbor's kid involved in this imaginary treasure hunt, is beyond me."

Aunt Caroline looked at Pam with wide, wondering eyes. Pam winked back at her. Emboldened, Aunt Caroline stiffened her spine, tilted her chin up, and said firmly, "I heard them say it. I heard them clearly say they were hiding something, and they were hiding it in *this house*. Our very own parents. I'm sure of it. I know what I heard."

"And what about the other house in West Cape May?" Maddy interjected. "*That's* really there."

"No one said the old house wasn't split up!" Mrs. Van den Burgh barked. "That's not under dispute. So you've found the other half. Great! Go tell it to the Cape May Historical Society! Big deal! But we're not going traipsing around on someone else's property. It's illegal. Besides, if there were anything there, it would be their property now anyway. Let them have it!"

At this, the rest of them exploded. A chorus of loud rebuttals of "Come on!" and "What?" and "Are you kidding?" overlapped each other.

Pam felt absolutely deflated. All that work, for nothing. She thought of the afternoon they explored the hot and horrible attic, and the time spent reading all those dumb books in the study, and then the completely accidental discovery of the garage at the end of that exhausting bike chase. All of that was just going to be dismissed as nothing? Just like that? Even if there wasn't a treasure, they had been on to something and they should follow it through. And too, maybe the historical society *would* like to know about what they discovered. It was just the thing that they put in those little guidebooks for tourists, Pam thought with satisfaction, suddenly feeling a lot better. At any rate, they should at least finish what they started.

With this determination in mind, Pam stood up abruptly, nearly sending the other two into a heap at the other end of the swing.

Ignoring Maddy's and Zara's cries of irritation, she said, "I'm going to get my parents. I'm going to tell them more about what I saw. Maybe *they'll* help me investigate." And she started down the porch steps.

"*You! You!* Help *you* investigate! *What?*" Mrs. Van den Burgh exploded, rising up from her seat just as abruptly.

Pam turned around with an expression of complete innocence. "Yes. I'll get them to take me over to West Cape May instead. They love these things. My mom especially. She's been dying to help out."

"Now wait just a minute, young lady. This is *our* mystery. Anything involving this house is strictly *our* business."

"But the garage has nothing to do with this house. That's what you just said," Pam argued, turning Mrs. Van den Burgh's reasoning around on her. "Besides, you keep saying there is no treasure. So there really is no mystery anyway."

Mrs. Van den Burgh's eyes narrowed as she looked at Pam steadily, her face reddening as she scrambled for a response.

"What I've been saying," she began testily, "is that that man's garage is not for us to poke around in. It's *his property*."

"Exactly." Pam turned back around toward home.

"However," the old woman bellowed, "that does not mean that we shouldn't at least ask him if we *can* have a look around." And with that, she scrambled down the porch steps before the others even knew what she was about, and ran toward her car.

"Last one in is a rotten egg!" the old woman further taunted Pam as she bustled toward the Mercedes.

"Oh, *brother*!" Pam exclaimed, as the others scrambled down the porch steps in a hurry. Maddy and Zara got to the car first, practically dragging Aunt Caroline. They headed for the back seat, leaving Pam to the front where Mrs. Van den Burgh was already revving the engine.

"Oh, *brother*!" Pam said again as she ran around the front of the car, got in, and barely closed the door before the old woman was backing out the drive, running over plants as she went.

As the back end of the car swerved out into the road, Pam gripped the seat and wondered if her parents wouldn't have been a better choice after all.

"Now," the old woman said to her forcefully, "you show us the way."

Yet despite her order, it seemed as if Mrs. Van den Burgh was stubbornly determined to find her own route. Pam had to shout out the directions as if to a deaf person, and soon lost all sense that she was speaking to an older person, a situation usually requiring a degree of manners. "Right. No, *right*! Left. Left! *Left*!" she would yell at the top of her lungs, as the older woman seemed to insist on doing the opposite of whatever she said. They finally arrived at the garage with one last shouted "*Stop*!" from Pam, who was by now thoroughly exhausted, and wishing with all her might that she could just ditch these nutty neighbors.

The garage mechanic looked up as the car came to its loud and abrupt halt before his driveway, and, wiping his hands with a cloth, started toward them.

"So, what seems to be the trouble?" He looked pleasant enough, and when everyone crowded around him and started talking at once, he tilted his head back and laughed.

"Whoa, whoa, whoa, one at a time." He grinned at them, and looked at the car appreciatively. He directed his gaze toward Mrs. Van den Burgh.

Boy, is he going to be disappointed it has nothing to do with the car, Pam thought. But instead the man said, "I'm sorry to disappoint you, but I don't work on foreign cars. Strictly American. But she's a beaut. A real beaut. What seems to be the trouble?"

Mrs. Van den Burgh sniffed haughtily and said, "Don't be absurd. I have a mechanic. Do you think I'd let just anyone work on this car?"

At this the man raised his eyebrows. Sensing that Mrs. Van den Burgh was potentially jeopardizing their mission, the rest of them started talking at once.

"No, we're not here about a car."

"We want to have a look around your garage."

"We're looking for a treasure, and we think it might be here."

Surprisingly, the man laughed again, and put his hands up in the air. "*What*? Please, one at a time! Now what is it you want?"

Much to Pam's surprise and annoyance, Maddy took up the explanation. But since she explained their mission well, even apologizing for any inconvenience, Pam looked at her admiringly when she finished, nodded, and said, "Yeah, that's right."

The man looked at them in amazement. "Are you kidding me? This is the most bizarre request anyone's ever pulled into this garage with. I can't let you wander around this property. Are you crazy?" This he directed toward the two older women, as if they should know better. But Mrs. Van den Burgh's attention seemed to have suddenly shifted to the surrounding trees, and Aunt Caroline just stood there blinking.

"But we promise we won't hurt anything. We just

want to prove that this garage was part of the other house," Maddy continued. "That way, even if we don't find the treasure, we'll have found *something*."

"And if we do prove that this was part of the other house, we're going to notify the Cape May Historical Register," Pam added. "They might even put that in tourist brochures, you know, as one of those little facts tourists like to read about on vacation."

"Harrumph. Yes. A little publicity might even help this place," Mrs. Van den Burgh said, looking around.

Before the man could react to the older woman's slight, they all jumped in with a chorus of "please, please, pleeeeze, pleeeeeze!" to the point where he looked like he was wavering.

"But a garage isn't safe for kids," he tried to reason with them. "It's also my business. I have tools, people's cars, and lots of things that are heavy, or just plain dangerous. Besides, what exactly are you looking for? I mean, what's all this about a treasure? And why on earth do you think it's here? What made you pick my garage?" the man asked logically.

"It's nonsense, that's what it is," Mrs. Van den Burgh interjected with spirit. "But these nutcrackers keep insisting on it."

"I'm right," Aunt Caroline murmured, "I'm right. I know I am."

"Nonsense," was Mrs. Van den Burgh's terse reply.

"What we're looking for to begin with," Pam began, exasperated at having to once again save the situation, "is any clues to the building that prove it was built *with* the other house. I've already noticed that the windows are the same. And that's why we're here." She explained what she had seen the previous day riding by, and what it was about the windows that made her think about their similarity to the windows on her neighbor's house. As she explained the architectural features of the two houses, the man listened with fascination. He was clearly impressed.

"So," Pam continued, "what we need to know is if this house ever had a cupola?"

"A what?"

Pam explained. The mechanic nodded his head in comprehension, but denied ever having seen such a thing. "I've had this garage and house" he nodded toward the little house that sat next door "for just two years. This is pretty much how it was when I bought it. I haven't even had time to clean up the junk out back, I've been so busy getting the business up and running. But this is a new roof. Put on by the guy who sold me the place. There's nothing up there."

They all looked up at the roof. It was hard, even for Pam, to imagine it any other way than brand new like it was. But she remained undaunted, and decided to press her luck with the man's softening stance toward their looking around. "Well," she began carefully, "how about if you show us around. That way you won't have to worry about us getting into trouble." She looked up at him and grinned.

The man threw his head back and laughed heartily. "Oh, you're good, you're really good."

Chapter Twenty

So the garage owner, who introduced himself as Paul, agreed to show them around, shaking his head with amusement as he started toward the garage doors. But before she moved to join the rest of them, Mrs. Van den Burgh motioned to Pam.

"What's all this about the windows?" She was referring, of course, to Pam's only clue connecting the two houses. Clearly she had not been listening carefully the first time Pam explained about their similarity while sitting on her front porch.

Pam pointed up to the garage roof where a second story would have been if the inside of the garage hadn't been entirely hollowed out. The others waited while Pam pointed out the features of the dormer windows that were identical to the one's on the third floor of Mrs. Van den Burgh's and Aunt Caroline's summer home. She noted their criss-crossing panes, and insisted that they were unusual on Victorian houses.

"But it's a new roof!" the older woman said.

"Yes, but the windows weren't changed," asserted Pam confidently. "You see how old they are, and how old the wood and the panes look. And besides, no one would build tall and narrow dormer windows on a new building these days," she said with authority.

"What?" the old woman practically shouted. "And exactly how do you know that?"

Pam shrugged. "I just know. I know houses. I've grown up with them."

Mrs. Van den Burgh looked at Pam steadily, then turned toward the others with pursed lips. "Well, well, let's go. We don't have all day. Let's get a move on."

Hearing this, Paul shook his head again, and led them in. As soon as they were inside, everyone looked up at the ceiling. But there was nothing there to see. There wasn't even anything to show that there had ever been a second story. The ceiling slanted upward at the front and back, meeting in a point that ran the length of the building. There was no sign of a trap door, or any feature at all indicating a cupola. Only the dormer windows looked odd and out of place, each jutting out from the slanted ceiling with a window seat that no one could even see, let alone sit on.

Paul pointed to them. "Since you're interested in the windows, I suppose it doesn't hurt to tell you that the previous owner liked them too. He said they let in a lot of light."

"How long did he have this place? Did he remodel it?" Pam asked.

"I have no idea how long he had it. I never thought about it. I suppose that's on the deed. But he did remodel. And apparently he did it himself, and was very proud of it. He even installed those big double garage doors."

They all looked at the doors. As if they reminded her of somewhere she'd rather be, Zara, who had been looking around the filthy garage with disgust, yawned loudly, and said, "Grandmother, I am going to sit in the car." She strode off quickly, as if to avoid further contamination.

Mrs. Van den Burgh pursed her lips even further.

The garage held no surprises. It was dirty, and full of cars, car parts, tires, tools, and all manner of machinery. Pam glanced quickly around, while Aunt Caroline watched Pam, ever hopeful.

"What about the back yard? Can we go have a look around there?"

Paul hesitated. "It's even more hazardous back there. It's a junkyard. There are whole rusting cars back there, more tires, wood and cinder blocks left over from some building project, even an old doghouse. I just haven't had a chance to get to any of it yet," he said ruefully.

Pam said, "We won't climb onto anything, or get into anything dangerous. Let's just have a look, please?"

"Well, at this point I'm not sure what you're going

to find that'll help you, but let's have a try," Paul said.

He led them out back.

"See," he said, indicating the mess. "I sure do have my work cut out for me."

He wasn't exaggerating. Under the canopy of a large maple tree lay a great mass of junk. And there were, indeed, whole rusting shells of vehicles that it was very hard to imagine had ever been on the road. The interior of the garage looked neat as a pin compared to this.

Maddy stood looking at the yard with her arms clasped around her back as usual, an expression of complete contentment on her face. She tilted her head and said to Pam, "Aren't you glad cleaning this mess up isn't one of your chores?" She nodded her head vigorously, as if agreeing with herself that it would, indeed, be the worst chore ever.

Of all of them, only Maddy still seemed cheerful. She was walking around the yard, weaving in and around piles of junk as if this was one of the most interesting excursions of her summer. Pam, on the other hand, was surveying the mess with a critical eye, moving her head this way and that, unsure what to do next, while Aunt Caroline, her sister, and Paul stood at the edge of the yard. It seemed as if everything depended on her. And yet she had no idea what to even look for. What should she do?

Suddenly, Maddy shouted, "Hey, look at this old doghouse! Neat! Come and see!"

Pam roused her attention from her aggravation and disappointment at being on a fool's errand, one she was responsible for no less, and carefully dodged junk on her way over to where Maddy stood, to look at what she was pointing to on the ground.

Pam looked down at a small, wooden structure that lay in several pieces on top of a bed of splintered glass and tried to summon up interest.

"See," Maddy said, "it even had windows. My dog would love that. Imagine, a doghouse with windows. I wonder how it got so broken up?"

"Yeah," Pam said without much interest. "I wonder. It's so smashed it looks as if it had been thrown from the roof."

They both laughed and looked at the piece of junk at their feet. Then, in slow motion and simultaneously, their heads rose until they were looking each other in the eye. Both of their mouths dropped open, and they looked back down at the broken remains of what they both knew had never, ever, been a doghouse.

So excited her hands were shaking, Pam jiggled the broken cupola and tried to turn it over. Something rustled underneath, and slithered away.

Maddy's scream sent Paul and Mrs. Van den Burgh

scurrying over. Paul looked shaken as he asked Maddy what happened.

"Nothing," she said giggling sheepishly. "When Pam tried to lift the cupola, something underneath made noise, and, well. . ." She giggled again.

"Tried to lift the what?" Mrs. Van den Burgh barked just as Aunt Caroline joined them. "What did you say?"

Maddy couldn't get it out fast enough. She was so excited at their discovery that her teeth were chattering as she explained how they'd both been looking at it as the old "doghouse" that Paul had referred to, when suddenly they realized that it was a cupola, and that it was, in fact, the cupola from the roof of the garage.

Mrs. Van den Burgh just stood there with her mouth open, while her sister started hopping up and down, saying over and over, "She was right! She was right! She was right!"

Paul, on the other hand, had been watching Pam unsuccessfully try to pull the broken structure upright. Nearly as excited as she was, he grabbed a hold of it, and pulled. But the movement was obviously too much for the thing, and the remains of the cupola broke apart. Now all four sides lay flat on the ground, and the structure's roof lay upside down, its interior exposed.

Aunt Caroline and the girls gasped.

Gold stars against a midnight blue background.

It was the absolute proof that Pam had been right; the absolute proof that this garage had once been attached to the larger house at the other end of town, and that for some reason, when the house was moved from South Cape May, this section of it had been settled here. Aunt Caroline was beside herself.

Only Paul and Mrs. Van den Burgh didn't understand the significance of the painting. As Pam, Maddy, and Aunt Caroline explained what they'd seen on the ceiling of their own cupola in town, Paul whistled.

"Well, I guess this *will* interest the historical society. It's a cool story. And you know what?" he addressed Mrs. Van den Burgh cheerfully. "You're right. The publicity won't hurt. It won't hurt a bit. I think we should photograph the ceilings of these two cupolas as soon as possible. What do you say?"

But Mrs. Van den Burgh wasn't listening. She was shaking her head as these details came pouring in, clearly wrestling with irritation that everyone had been right. It seemed as if nothing could have annoyed her more. She asked Pam again, comprehending with some difficulty, "You mean, that one we have upstairs in our attic has this exact same painting?"

Pam giggled at the older woman's difficulties. "Well, they're not *exactly* the same. But it's the same idea, the same painting."

Maddy frowned. "What do you mean? They're exactly the same. Gold stars painted against a dark blue sky."

"Yes," Pam agreed patiently, "but this one is done right on the wood. The other one was painted on wall paper, or something. The surface was smoother."

"Are you kidding me? How you see these things is beyond me," Maddy said, shaking her head. "But it doesn't matter. That's just a dumb detail. What matters is that the same person painted both of them, for some weird reason."

"Yes. My mother," Mrs. Van den Burgh said simply.

The two girls glanced at her, expecting her to continue. But the older woman was lost in thought, and frowning.

"My mother," she said again quietly. Then, looking up, she added more firmly, "And from what I know of her, she always did things for a reason, and *never* overlooked details."

Both girls were quiet.

"And," Mrs. Van den Burgh continued, addressing Maddy, "everything we've found today has been the result of someone paying attention to details that most of us would consider "dumb" or beneath notice, which is what you really mean."

Pam flushed at the obvious compliment. But Maddy, always ready to oblige, nodded vigorously. "I know, I know. Pam's on the ball."

"That's putting it mildly," Mrs. Van den Burgh said wryly. "Let's go." Her voice had resumed its gruff texture. "We're not done."

She motioned to them to follow her, and they all went back around the garage to the front.

They thanked Paul profusely for allowing them to trespass, and Aunt Caroline agreed, as she pressed his hand, that he could come over to photograph the other cupola in a few days. "I mean, it's not a treasure," Paul said, "but it sure is neat all the same." Aunt Caroline blinked in response.

They got into the car, where Maddy related everything Zara had missed. Zara, naturally, took their adventure in stride, meaning, of course, that she didn't betray one ounce of interest or enthusiasm as she listened to Maddy's recital. Aunt Caroline was also in the back, looking alternately happy and sad, while Pam sat up front, thrilled at her discovery, but curious as to what Mrs. Van den Burgh had meant by "We're not done."

She looked over at the older woman, who was gripping the wheel, staring ahead thoughtfully.

Mrs. Van den Burgh turned to look at Pam. "You sure are one observant kid."

"I know!" Maddy exclaimed from the back seat.

"And do you believe that Pam saw that garage as we were riding by, chasing after Pam's stolen bike? She just recognized those windows, just like that!"

"Hm. Yes, that is amazing, especially now that we know she was right. But I wasn't referring to that."

All heads turned to look at the erect, gray-haired lady, suddenly alert to a new tone in her voice.

"What did you. . .Oh!. . ." Pam stopped, the light dawning. "You think there's something more. That's what you meant."

"Well, let me put it this way. The first thing we're going to do when we get back is hunt down a flashlight."

"No need," Pam said, pulling a small gadget out of her pocket. "This one's powerful." She flicked it on and off.

Mrs. Van den Burgh took one look at it, threw her head back, and howled with laughter.

Chapter Twenty-One

The ride back was quiet, grim, and determined. Those in the back seat weren't sure what was up, or in the case of Zara, didn't care. Pam, again sitting in the front, was concentrating hard on what might have inspired Mrs. Van den Burgh's complete change of attitude. For changed it certainly was. On the way over to West Cape May she'd behaved as if she was humoring a bunch of nutty kids on a wild goose chase. Now, she was deep in serious thought, so focused in fact, that she wasn't even giving Pam a hard time taking her directions. Pam glanced at her, wondering what on earth she was up to. She had no doubt that they were going up into the attic again. But for what?

Mrs. Van den Burgh discarded the car in the driveway as soon as she pulled in. She barked orders for them to follow her, and strode swiftly into the house.

They gathered in the hallway, unsure exactly what to do. Mrs Van den Burgh reappeared, and came toward them with a small knife in her hand.

They all stood there staring at her as she began to

ascend the stairs, none of them speaking, until one by one, they each followed her lead.

At the bottom of the second floor staircase, Mrs. Van den Burgh motioned to Pam to take the lead. "You've been up here recently," was all she said.

Pam dutifully stepped in front, her excitement mounting. At the attic door, Pam paused before opening it, and said, "We're going to have to open the attic windows again, or we'll never be able to breathe. Wait here for a second."

She opened the door, and they were hit once again with a suffocating blast of hot air. Pam stepped through, pulling out her flashlight. As she made her way over to a window, the others waited by the door. After opening just two windows, she came back and got the metal rod from behind the door.

"Here," she said, handing it to Mrs. Van den Burgh, "I'll hold the light while you hook it in the loop." She pointed to the metal loop in the ceiling.

Because she was so much taller than any of them, Mrs. Van den Burgh had no trouble with the hook. As soon as it was secure, she pulled hard on the rod, and the trap door came swinging down with a bang.

"Watch out! You'd better. . ." Pam started to say, but too late. The old woman had barely unfolded the attached stairs, before she was ascending them.

Mrs. Van den Burgh was so tall she only had to stand on the top step of the ladder to touch the ceiling of the cupola.

"Uh, huh," was all she said. The rest of them clustered below, on the attic floor, peering intently as the old woman wedged her knife under a corner edge of the paper that lined the cupola's ceiling.

It soon became apparent that only the edges were glued. As her knife slid around, loosening the old glue, the whole piece started to come off. Pam said, "See what I mean? The stars are painted on wall paper."

But even Maddy wasn't listening. She was staring in fascination as Mrs. Van den Burgh cut out the entire small ceiling that they had admired only the other day. Now the older woman had one thick square piece in her hands, the reverse side of which had caught her attention.

Suddenly, Pam remembered something. "But what about Paul?" she burst out.

"What about him?" Mrs. Van den Burgh said distractedly, still peering at the piece of wallpaper.

"We said he could photograph the ceiling! What do we do *now?*" an exasperated Pam asked.

"Well, we'll just stick it back up when we're done with it." And with that, she reversed her steps and came carefully back down the trapdoor stairs.

"So, what is it! What's on the wallpaper?" Maddy

cried excitedly, jumping up and down.

"She knows," Aunt Caroline calmly said. "She knows what's under the cupola."

"Well, what is it?" Zara cried impatiently.

Only Pam waited quietly while Mrs. Van den Burgh peeled a piece of very yellowed paper off the back of the wall paper. She carefully unfolded it, and held it closer to the light.

None of them could stand the suspense. Amid cries of "Well, what is it?" and "What's on it? What's the treasure?" the old woman suddenly threw her head back in laughter.

"Oh, good God, you'll never believe it! Oh good God, *I* can't believe it! Oh, she was a character, alright! Come on guys, let's go have a look at the treasure!"

Pam couldn't tell from the tone of her voice if she was being sarcastic or not. She was on the verge of feeling disappointed until the whole group, having made its way down to the second floor, was led into Aunt Caroline's bedroom.

"Well, Caroline," her older sister began, "you were right. I hate to say it, but you were right. You were right all along. There *is* a treasure. And you've been sleeping under it, every summer you spent in Cape May!"

Aunt Caroline's face registered a mixture of satisfaction and bafflement, as her eyes followed where her sister was pointing.

"See that?" Mrs. Van den Burgh asked all of them, pointing to the white chandelier over the bed. "That's it."

"That's it?" Maddy cried, trying not to sound disappointed.

"That piece of *junk*?" Zara cried in annoyance.

Aunt Caroline's eyes blinked furiously.

"What do you mean?" Pam asked, puzzled. "Isn't that just a china chandelier?"

Mrs. Van den Burgh was clearly enjoying this moment. "No. According to this diagram that is precisely what it is *not*, although that is what it is supposed to *appear* to be. In fact," she said, as she held the yellowed, fragile paper lower for them all to see, "it is a solid silver chandelier, most likely worth a heap of money."

All eyes looked up at the fabulously ornate, white chandelier. It looked so far from being any of the things it was supposed to be, that the group remained silent, still in doubt.

Pam broke the silence. "Silver? You mean it's *painted? Painted* white?"

Mrs. Van den Burgh nodded. "Once again, you're miles ahead of everyone. Look."

They all huddled around the paper, and sure enough, it was a sketch of the chandelier above. Around the drawing were many notes, in tiny, old fashioned handwriting.

"What does it say?" Maddy asked. "I can hardly read it."

"It appears to be directions for how it was covered in some sort of enamel, in addition to directions for taking it off without damaging the silver. All written by my mother."

"But why? Why would she do that? It makes no sense!" Pam exclaimed. "Why hide a beautiful object under all that gunk?"

"Well, for one, I have a feeling that this chandelier is quite a bit more than just an extraordinary piece of silver. But as to how she got it, and why it needed disguising," Mrs. Van den Burgh shrugged, "that, my dears, still remains a mystery."

Pam looked at the chandelier, now transformed in her mind into the phenomenally beautiful and rare thing that it was. "Solid silver. Solid silver," she repeated. "Can you imagine how much. . ." Her voice trailed off.

"Quite a bit, I'd say," the old woman answered her question. To Zara she said, "We'll have to call your mother immediately, you know. She'll know what to do. And now," Mrs. Van den Burgh said, turning to the rest of them, "let's all go out to dinner. All this excitement has given me quite the appetite!"

Chapter Twenty-Two

For over a week, everyone was caught up in the excitement of the find. Zara's mother, who worked for a famous auction house in New York, came down to Cape May as soon as Mrs. Van den Burgh had informed her of their discovery. Since Mrs. Annesley wasn't a silver expert, she brought with her someone who was, a co-worker from the auction house who would not only be able to remove the lacquered coating on the chandelier, but who might also be able to tell them all a bit more about the piece. Like, for instance, how much it was worth. *That* little detail had them all on the edge of their seats.

So the chandelier was carefully taken down from the ceiling and laid out on the dining room table where the expert worked on it like a surgeon handling a delicate operation. What emerged, slowly, from under his hands, was a thing of extraordinary beauty. The ornate design began to appear in gleaming silver out from under the thick, white coat like a snake shedding an unworthy skin. Every time Pam visited next door to see how it was coming along, she felt a wave of enormous pride at having been instrumental in recovering something so wonderful.

Her mother, on the other hand, needed serious consolation, which Pam happily offered in between giggles.

"Of all the luck!" Mrs. Fischer cried over and over again for days. "Of course, I'm proud of you, you little treasure hunter, you," she said, patting Pam's head. "But how typical! We scour the yard sales and antiques shops for hours on end and usually only come away with junk. And meanwhile these people have a kazillion dollar treasure right in their own home. Just *hanging* there! Ugh!"

Needless to say, Aunt Caroline was wandering around in a state of euphoria, looking a bit more dazed than usual. For years, she'd insisted that there was a treasure in their summer home, and for as many years her sister had dismissed the idea as "bonkers." But Aunt Caroline had stubbornly clung to her opinion, and she'd been right, after all. *Proven* right. She was so grateful to Pam, she beamed at her every time she saw her, and promised, *promised*, amid many blinks and shrugs, that she'd see a reward one day.

But then suddenly, things took a downward turn. The silver specialist, who had taken numerous photographs of the restoration process, had bad news. Apparently some of the photos which he had sent on to his boss at the auction house had caught the eye of a man who worked for the Art Loss Register. This man had requested some of the pictures of the chandelier in order to compare them with his data on the registry, which was a data base holding the records of thousands of stolen art works from around the world. The Art Loss Register was like the F.B.I. of the art world. And this man had bad news for everyone.

A chandelier, seemingly identical to the one just discovered in Cape May, was registered as a stolen work, last seen in a French Chateau just at the outbreak of World War II. It had been assumed either stolen by the occupying Germans, or else sent into hiding by the wealthy Jewish family who had owned it. Unfortunately, that meant that if it was indeed proven to be the same chandelier, Aunt Caroline, Mrs. Van den Burgh, and their brother would not be able to keep it. All they would be able to expect would be a finders fee, if that.

Naturally, everyone was dismayed at this news. Aunt Caroline blinked furiously as this new turn of events was explained over and over to her. Mrs. Van den Burgh simply went about the house bellowing "Hell's bells!" at the top of her lungs, while the three girls scrambled to figure out what war they were all talking about.

In the end, it looked like there was no answer immediately forthcoming as to why a chandelier, last known to have been hanging in a French chateau in the late 1930's, had ended up in Cape May, New Jersey, painted to look much less valuable than it was. Only Aunt Caroline and Mrs. Van den Burgh's mother had the answer, and she had died not long after she'd installed the chandelier in South Cape May, disguised as a piece of junk.

Naturally, Maddy thought it was "soooo romantic! Just think," she said to Pam as they were lazing about on the porch swing, "you found an *international* treasure. Amazing! Maybe there will be a reward, hand delivered by a French count!" And off she would drift into a misty daydream.

Zara, on the other hand, observing all that was going on from a lofty distance, appeared unconcerned and above it all, except for those moments when her grandmother would suddenly burst out with another "Our mother the art thief! Hell's bells!" Then the dark eyes would flicker to attention, dart toward her grandmother, and gaze steadily, only to once again settle on some distant object on the horizon.

Pam, of course, took an interested, but practical view, and remained unperturbed that things hadn't turned out quite the way they'd all hoped. After all, she'd still solved Aunt Caroline's mystery and found a real life treasure, one more valuable than anything even Maddy could have dreamt up. All in all, she was truly satisfied. Except for one thing.

She still hadn't called her friend Katy to confess her complete failure to uphold their agreement. It was embarrassing, and Pam squirmed at the thought of what she'd have to say. But after several conversations with her father about the importance of facing up to things, Pam finally summoned up the courage to call the camp. Her stomach did somersaults the whole time she waited for Katy to come on the line, so by the time she heard Katy's voice, Pam was so sick of feeling nervous, that she blurted out the whole story, hardly stopping for air—or a reaction. Finally she was done. She waited.

At the other end of the line, she heard muffled sounds, as if Katy was talking to someone else and holding her hand over the receiver.

"Katy! Are you there?" Pam yelled, annoyed. She began to repeat her story, more slowly this time, no longer caring how dumb it sounded. In the middle of her second recitation, she was sure that she heard laughing. Pam became indignant.

"What are you laughing for?" she bellowed. "Are you listening to me? Have you heard one word I said?"

What had previously sounded a bit like giggling now erupted into full fledged, hysterical laughter.

Pam was outraged. No longer caring if the old woman at *The Chocolate Pot* was Katy's grandmother or not, she threw all caution to the wind.

"That woman was *mean!*" she yelled. "She yelled at me for every single thing I did. And even for stuff I didn't do. Who is she?" Pam demanded, full of indignation. "And why didn't you warn me about her?"

Katy's hysteria had mostly subsided, and so, between lingering giggles, Katy explained that the old woman was just "some old lady" who'd been working at *The Chocolate Pot* for years and years and *years*.

"You mean, she's not your *grandmother?*" Pam screeched, not sure whether to be glad or even madder.

"Heck no!" And Katy went on to wholeheartedly agree with Pam on her assessment of the old woman's character. "She's a witch, alright," Katy matter-of-factly pronounced. "No doubt about it. Full-fledged, one hundred percent witch. I don't know how you lasted as long as you did. If my parents didn't own the place, I'd have quit long ago."

This left Pam speechless. Then it dawned on her.

"You *knew!* You knew all along! You *escaped!* And stuck me with the ogre! Aaaagh!" she yelled into the phone. "Just you wait till you come back, Katy! Just you wait!" And Pam slammed down the phone, silencing the renewed peals of laughter at the other end.

"AAAAAGH!" was all she said, stomping off in the direction of next door. She was so mad she felt that she could even take on Mrs. Van den Burgh. Maybe even join her in a few of those "Hell's bells!"

Chapter Twenty-Three

It was their last night all together, and they were sitting in the large living room, having just had dinner. The chandelier had been wrapped up, and the next morning Zara's mother and Mrs. Van den Burgh were off to New York to research the ownership problem further. So far, it looked as if it were going to be reunited with its French family, but for now it was Mrs. Van den Burgh's responsibility.

Zara and Aunt Caroline were going to remain in Cape May until the end of vacation. Maddy was positively thrilled at this.

"Yeah," Pam said, "but what are we all going to do *now?*"

Everyone laughed. Pam had been invited as their guest of honor for the evening, for, they all agreed, no matter who finally got the treasure, the hunt sure had been fun, and it wouldn't have happened without Pam. Even so, she had spent the evening being relentlessly teased by Mrs. Van den Burgh. The mood was happy and everyone was excited for different reasons—all except Zara, of course, who had just sat there sulking throughout the entire meal.

Pam had eyed her with increasing irritation, wondering how she could just push her food around her plate like that and not be tempted just to give in for once and shovel in a mouthful. But it didn't happen, and no sooner was dinner concluded, than Zara swiftly disappeared upstairs without a word to anyone.

Naturally, this outraged Pam, for as the evening's guest of honor, it seemed like a direct insult to her.

As she sat there in the living room, extremely annoyed but still bantering with Mrs. Van den Burgh as well as she could, she saw Maddy get up and leave the room. She was about to protest in annoyance, when Aunt Caroline got up from her chair and came to stand, winking and blinking, in front of her.

Pam felt embarrassed as the older woman just stood there staring at her, her mouth opening and closing as if she were trying to say something. She figured that Aunt Caroline was simply trying to thank her for the zillionth time for finding the treasure, but just as she was about to respond, Maddy returned, wheeling into the living room a brightly painted bike, decorated with ribbons and streamers, and with a huge bow perched on the handle bars.

Pam's mouth dropped open in astonishment. She got up from her chair, and slowly moved toward the bike in a daze, saying quietly, "It's green, it's green!"

Then, dropping to her knees in awe, she inspected every wonderful detail of her fabulous present, delivering a running commentary on its finer points to Maddy, whose excitement was nearly as great as Pam's.

Aunt Caroline finally found words.

"It's a gift. For all you've done," she said, her blue eyes blinking happily.

"I'm sure she knows that Caro, but thanks anyway," her sister commented drily.

Pam jumped up and first bear-hugged Maddy, and then Aunt Caroline, leaving the elderly lady somewhat breathless, but still beaming. Then she turned to Mrs. Van den Burgh with her hand firmly outstretched, ready to give a hearty handshake.

Mrs. Van den Burgh looked down at the hand she'd been offered, and threw her head back and laughed. She then obliged Pam with a firm handshake, saying, "Believe me, kiddo, you've done more for us than we've done for you by giving you this bike. I have a feeling that at some point we'll be adding to that gift," she said, her eyes twinkling.

But Pam couldn't have cared less about any gift other than the one she had in her hands, and she couldn't wait to get it home and lock it up safely. Tomorrow was going to be a glorious day.

She said her grateful goodbyes to the two sisters and to Zara's mother, and then gleefully wheeled the bike, accompanied by Maddy, out the front door.

But not even the unexpected thrill of a brand new bike could quench her thorough annoyance with Maddy's friend for insulting her like that. So no sooner had she and Maddy rounded the hedge dividing the two properties, than Pam exploded.

"What a snot!"

"What?" Maddy asked, bewildered.

"A snot! A snot! A darned snot!" Pam said with vehemence. "I hate her!"

Maddy looked at Pam thoughtfully, finally comprehending who she meant.

"Why do you say that?"

"What?" asked Pam, incredulous. "Are you kidding? She just went off to her room without saying goodnight, thanks, or anything. Ugh!"

They paused in the Fischer's driveway beside Pam's house. Maddy turned to face Pam. Even in the twilight, Pam could see Maddy's face clearly. She had never looked so serious.

"You think she's a snot just because she wasn't downstairs with the rest of us?" Maddy asked calmly.

"You bet!" Pam cried forcefully. She wanted to add that she also thought Zara was a snot in general, but couldn't think of how to say it without hurting Maddy's feelings. After all, strange as it still seemed to Pam, the snot was Maddy's best friend.

"You're kidding, right?" Maddy continued. "You think her behavior was because of you? Are you nuts? Don't you see? Don't you get it?" Maddy paused. "She hasn't heard from her mother all summer so far, not even one phone call. But as soon as her mom hears there's a valuable antique down here, she's actually here, in person, just like that." Maddy snapped her fingers. "Think about it. What would that tell you?"

Pam swallowed hard, and attempted to say something, but nothing came out. She looked down at her feet, suddenly feeling incredibly awkward.

"It would tell you," Maddy continued, "that you weren't as important as some dumb antique. That's why she left the group and went upstairs. Because she knows that that stupid chandelier means more to her mother than *she* does."

And with that, Maddy turned and walked down the drive toward the little cottage.

Pam just stood there, watching her walk away, filled with shame and embarrassment. Why had she thought it was all about her? She looked at her house, all lit up, and at the garden, the source of so many of her complaints. She thought of how it reflected so much of her parents, their hobbies and passions (obsessions, where her mother was concerned). But no matter what, none of it had ever seemed to be more important than she was. None of it. She was at the center of it all–and never, ever did she give that a second thought.

She thought of Zara, upstairs in that big house, feeling unimportant and pushed entirely to the side. Less important than an antique. Less important than her mother's interests. Pam felt sick at the thought, and experienced a sudden sensation of loneliness that she'd never felt before. She shivered.

Suddenly, the sound of clanging pots pierced the air. Someone was in the kitchen.

"Mom! Dad!" Pam ran with her new bike toward the kitchen steps in a rush of emotion, and, after hastily propping the bike up against the side of the house, rushed inside.

CPSIA information can be obtained
at www.ICGtesting.com
Printed in the USA
BVHW070441180719
553742BV00009B/191/P